I0676088

THE
SPLINTERED
LANDS

ISABELLA LAIRD

Copyright © 2024 Isabella Laird
All rights reserved.

"The plague is an infection of utmost importance. It takes hold of people, and transforms them into something different. Something monstrous. All Purists should be aware of their most prominent traits.

Many plague will have a limp, wound, wart, or other unusual growth/injury. A natural injury should heal in no more than six months. Any longer lasting injuries are a sign of the plague.

Strange behavior is another common trait. All individuals should know not to repeat themselves, and how to properly respond to questions. A failure to do so is an indicator of plague activity.

Plague are also known to take up strange disguises. White streaks in one's hair, crooked noses, or unusual eye colors are all common examples.

All Purists, be on the watch for any individuals with these traits. Your judgment is paramount, and it is up to you to decide whether someone is a plague or person. Tread carefully."

PART 1: WILLOW ROOTS

998 AD

CHAPTER 1

MIL

Mil must have been too preoccupied, because the next thing he knew, a fist was colliding with his cheek. He spat out a mixture of blood and spit, falling to the ground as his cheek throbbed. His mind rattled, trying to piece together the series of events that had befallen him.

He had been observing the natural beauty of the temple, and then, he was on the ground. Forced onto the ground. The realization hit him too late to save him from the next blow, a kick that landed on the right side of his stomach.

Pain shot through him again, and he lunged up to meet his attackers. It was two other acolytes, both bigger than him. The first one had dark black hair, while the other had dirty blond locks that fell onto his face. Whoever they were, they weren't in his class.

"Stop it!" The two only gave giddy looks to each other, moving apart to approach him. They were trying to close him in, and it was working. He could either run to the temple and hope the doors were unlocked, or fight. Neither of the options sounded appealing.

He couldn't remember the last time he had a fight, and he quaked as he stepped back. They shouldn't have been attacking him, but these two had no care for the codes. He didn't even know why they were doing this.

"We can work this out! If it's something you want, I can get it to you, I swear." The first bully chuckled at that, approaching at a more rapid pace.

"As if, shortstuff. Not our fault you wandered away from the temple!"

Mil opened his mouth to reply, but before he could the second one leapt forward. His fist collided with his skull, and he was once again knocked down. This time though, they didn't give him any time to get up, and began to hammer his body with kicks and punches.

Mil wrapped his arms around himself to protect what he could, holding in a scream as his body cracked beneath the pressure. His ribs felt like they were about to pop out, but soon enough each blow blurred into the next. The pain was too constant to ignore.

That was, until it all stopped. No new pressure was added, and after a few seconds, he dared to peek his head up. The second bully was holding his arms in defense, as someone landed punch after punch on him.

Mil could make out the attacker, a tan skinned man, and someone the size of his bullies. When the first one spun around, trying to land a blow, Mil shot up, a new beat within him. Adrenaline coursed through his veins, and he curled his hands into a fist.

Mil collided with the first bully, who toppled to the ground under his weight. It was only for a moment before he found himself thrown off, but he had the bullies attention. Mil danced circles around him, doing his best to avoid anything that was sent his way.

A few landed nonetheless, but he managed to lead the bully in circles. The bully was so distracted, he failed to see the shadow behind him, until something crashed upon his head. He let out a yell, falling back to his friend.

Mil turned to get a good look at the man supporting him. He recognized him, although they had never spoken before. Bolios, one of the other kids in his class, and one of the strongest ones to boot.

"Lay off, mate! We were just roughing around with him." One of the bullies cried out. Mil was shocked, because he wasn't trying to engage Bolios. He was trying to get him to leave. Were they really that scared of him?

"I could say the same to you. Wouldn't want to have to bash that pretty little face in!"

The bullies didn't need further warning, and they took off running towards the woods. Mil debated shouting, and warning them not to go, but he decided not to after his ribs groaned in protest again. If they were lucky, they'd find their ways back.

"Thank you?" He didn't know how to praise his savior, who could have left him to be beat. With no Purists around to enforce the rules, they could have gotten away with anything. He should have been more careful.

"Don't mention it! They got what was coming to them, beating up another acolyte." He scrutinized Mil, looking at him from top to bottom. Once he finished, a wide smile broke across his face. "What's your name? Rilt, or something?"

"No!" He gawked at the imitation. "It's Mil. And you're Bolios, right?" Bolios nodded in reply, surveying the area around him.

"Yep! And looking at those bruises, I think we need to get you back, Mil. You could use a trip to the healers."

Mil wanted to go, as the searing pain started to creep back in him, but he knew he couldn't. "We'll need to tell the tutor first, or she'll mark us tardy."

"Her? She won't do anything."

Mil shot him a look, and Bolios fell silent. Mil wasn't about to start playing hooky.

Bolios led the way back to the temple, and he limped behind him. He now prayed those bullies wouldn't return, because he'd rather avoid facing their torment again.

The doors creaked open as they walked through the halls, and Mil couldn't help but have his gaze wander to Bolios. Why had he helped him? If anything, having one less acolyte to compete with wouldn't have hurt.

Bolios snapped his head towards him, his eyebrows raised and mouth quirked up. "Why all the staring? Now I know I'm good looking but-."

"No!" Mil threw his hands up and started to wave them, an uncomfortable sensation running through him. "I just wondered why you would help me... it isn't like it benefited you at all."

Bolios let out a sigh, patting his chest. "I didn't know you thought so lowly of me!" He flashed Mil a smile, "Of course I'd help a classmate! What do you think this is, a death camp?"

"Well, no." Mil didn't know what to say past that. He wasn't used to his classmates being so eager to help, but Bolios was right. Shouldn't they all be helping each other?

At last, they came to their classroom, and he could hear the loud voices of students, and the even louder voice of the tutor behind the door.

As they opened the first door, they were greeted to a room full of sitting acolytes, and a tutor at the front. She was drawing on a board with a piece of charcoal, her voice drilling on about the purist code.

"A good Purist is to follow their commander's orders exactly. If they are not done correctly, then our mission is halted another day. Now, can anyone tell me what the rankings are?"

Mil opened his mouth to interject, but others were already speaking up.

"A platoon is led by a General, ma'am, and every General has a second. Skilled generals will be promoted to be one of the commander's disciples."

The teacher went to speak again, but Bolios apparently had less patience than Mil did. He thumped his foot until everyone in the room shifted to him.

"Hey! Teach! We're over here."

The tutor gave them both a stern look, and Mil was about ready to sink into the floor. Why did Bolios have to address her like that? Now they were screwed.

"Bolios and Mil. Both terribly late to class, and with attitude it seems. I'm sure you two have an explanation for your tardiness?"

"Hey! It wasn't our fault. Two boys from the higher grades came and tried to start a brawl wi-."

"You fought two other acolytes!? And you come here with no shame?"

Mil tried to butt in, his limbs shaky from the accusation. He couldn't get a tick on his record so soon, and not when he was attacked! "We didn't start anything. I was attacked by them, and Bolios helped me!"

"If that's true, then why didn't you get a Purists assistance, hm? Instead you took the fight into your own hands!"

"We were defending ourselves! It's not our fault that all the Purists were fooling around!"

A deafening silence hit the room, and the tutor stared down Bolios, watching as his confidence deflated like a balloon. The tutor stepped up towards Bolios, ruler in hand as she looked up to the boy.

A loud crack sounded about, the ruler smashing off his face. Mil was frozen, shivering from the mere thought of that happening to him. Bolios didn't react, but through his clenched teeth, Mil could tell the blow hurt.

"Let me be clear, boy. As an acolyte, we may strip you of your status at any moment! And if I hear another word from you, I won't hesitate to put the order in."

Words died on Bolios's lips as he stared on, daring not to test the warning of the tutor. Mil debated speaking up, but he knew he couldn't. Bolios shouldn't have spoken up.

A few of the other acolytes started to giggle and whisper amongst themselves, and Mil felt his heart drop. When would this train wreck ever end?

"It seems you boys haven't forgotten all of your respect. Take this to heart class on how not to act."

She turned her attention back to the two of them, snapping her fingers. Mil followed her fingers with his gaze, about ready to disappear into whatever place he came from. He just wanted this to be over with.

"Mil, as punishment, you'll be assigned to messenger duty. But first, see the healers, those bruises are only growing."

"As for you, Bolios, we'll be talking in my office. Now, shoo, I have a class to teach if you can't tell."

Mil gave a passing glance to Bolios, before hobbling in the direction of the healers bay. He wanted to stay and try to even things out, but something told him the decision was final. He had tried so hard to be the perfect acolyte, and now it was crumbling in front of his face.

He listened to his steps as he walked down the hard floors, wondering when things went so wrong. What had he even done to get on another acolyte's bad side?

He paused outside the healers door, his head hung low as he peered inside. He couldn't see much inside the bay, and he had to assume it was empty. He would have all of the healer's attention.

He debated moving away, before the door flung open, and a man opened it. "Oh you poor boy! Look at those bruises." He reached his hand out, patting the roughened skin as Mil flinched.

"Come inside, we better get you patched up!"

Mil didn't get a word out before he was pulled in and sat on a bed, the healer reaching to grab a string of bandages, and throwing things into a bowl.

"Now how did you get those wounds, acolyte? Did you fall down the hill?" The healer's face fell as he turned, now holding a bowl of golden liquid. Mil let his shoulders fall.

"I got hit. By another acolyte." He cringed as he expected the healer to scold him, but instead, he stood up straight, his face soured.

"Good lord! Who was it? I'll make sure they are punished severely."

Mil didn't know who the two were, and he didn't want the healer to bother. His tutor already made a decision.

"I don't know. Can you wrap my wounds?" He grabbed the bowl from the healer, slurping down the bitter liquid. It had a sweet aftertaste, at the least.

The healer stopped, but obliged, asking Mil to raise his tunic as he wrapped the bandages around his ribs.

"My names Melvon. If you ever remember, just come to my office?"

Mil weakly nodded, "Do you know where the messengers quadrant is? I have duties there."

"Take the hallway down, and do the second left. I would take you there, but I need to keep my office manned."

Mil got up, feeling the drum in his ribs as he walked out. He could have stayed longer, but he felt undeserving of the healer's presence.

After all, a guilty Purist deserved more than what he got.

CHAPTER 2

ALYX

"Please come, Adrienne. You can't stay here any longer." Auntie was near wailing as the rest of the family looked on, Alyx was backed up against her mothers side, trying to decipher the twists and turns of everyone's faces.

"We can't leave our home, Natalie. What if he comes back? He'll find an empty home!" Her mother retorted back, and grandma stepped up, scanning over the two, her mouth drooping.

"He isn't coming back, Adrienne. It's been more than four years. Mother, please, knock some sense into her! We can't leave her and Alyx here alone."

Grandma was silent, as she usually was, smacking her cane around as she paced the area. "'Tis true, Adrienne. We already heard word of the purists approach. We ain't risking staying here any longer. What will happen to that girl of yours?"

Alyx tilted her head, now knowing they were referring to her. Why would grandma be talking about her? Although she didn't know what they were discussing, she could feel the intensity of the conversation, like a beating vein.

"It wasn't real! You should know that, mom. I can't believe you're all abandoning the town over this! This was our home!"

The family all looked at one another, muttering amongst themselves. Alyx puffed up her cheeks, crossing her arms to resemble their body language. Her mother gave her a firm look in response.

"At least let Alyx come with us, dear. If the purists do come, she will be in harm's way. Evalkyr will treat her far kinder."

Her mothers face widened at that, and she stomped up, right into the face of the person who suggested such a thing. "Alyx is not leaving! We're both staying here. If you want to leave, then do it."

Auntie turned to Alyx, her arms outstretched, but her face not matching the happy attitude she portrayed. "Alyx, come here. Auntie needs to talk to you."

Alyx went to waddle over, but a large shape got between her and her aunt. It was her mother, and her face exuded nothing but fury. Alyx jumped back at the mere sight of it, hiding behind the nearest object.

"Enough! Go already. You aren't taking my daughter away from me!"

An uncle emerged from the crowd, pushing and shoving as his fists curled. "You're being an idiot, Adrienne! You and your daughter are going to have early graves because of your stubbornness."

Grandma turned, smacking the uncle with her cane, her lips flexing as her wrinkles churned. She then looked back to her mother. "If ye wish to stay, Adrienne, there is nothing we can do to stop you. I pray for your safety."

At that, the family shifted, some looking back, others marching away. But soon enough, every member except Alyx and her mother were engulfed, becoming a black mass that got farther and farther away.

"When are they coming back, mama?"

Her mother looked at her, a single tear falling as she spun around. "They aren't going to be coming back." She spat, bitterness seeping off her tongue, and Alyx froze.

"Grandma... is never coming back?"

Her mothers face softened, and she shook her head. "Eventually, Alyx. Just follow me."

Her mother yanked on her hand, pulling Alyx through the market as she looked left and right. People were setting up their shops, trading, and discussing amongst one another. A wide berth opened as they passed, and she was left staring.

Alyx was led all the way back to their house, where she was placed in the corner, staring at the large frame in front of her. In it, a robed man was painted on, standing next to her mother, and a whole set of candles were lit around it.

Alyx had stopped asking about it when her mother would break out into tears over the picture, and start throwing things around in the house. Instead, she tried to make up her own ideas of what the frame could be.

She thought the man was actually a prince, and he had come to bless her mother with gold. And one day, they'd all go back to his palace, eat the grandest of food, and dance until their legs fell out.

When her mother turned around, she shifted her gaze elsewhere, not wanting to be caught staring at it. Her mother was holding a basket now, and plopped the heavy item into Alyx's arms. She almost tumbled forward from the weight.

"Alyx, I need you to go up to Mr. Porters stand. Gather as much fruit as you can fit in here. Alright?"

Alyx flicked her white hair, not muttering any kind of response, causing her mother to groan. Next thing she knew, she was out the door, basket in hand, and street in front of her. She didn't know which way Mr. Porter's stand was, but she resolved to keep moving.

She let her little legs carry her down the mud and gravel path, her shoes sticking to the ground as she tried. She looked to the carts and large men walking by her, then to the fenced in cows on the other side. Were any of them Mr. Porter?

Instead, her eyes were drawn to a woman, with a circle of kids surrounding her, and her voice raised as she spoke. With her attention stolen, Alyx trotted over, still holding the basket as she listened in, pushing her way through the crowd.

The woman was missing the front half of her arm, and she looked at each of the kids, a grin on her face. "Have any of you heard the tale of The Great Parting?"

The other kids shook their heads, and Alyx followed in suit, her gaze now transfixed as she listened. She loved stories, but mother always refused to tell them to her anymore.

"You see, there were once creatures that ruled these lands. And not a simple beast or tiger, but something even smarter than us! This creature had the body of an eagle, and the legs of a lion, and it was bigger than any horse."

Alyx peeked her head through, staring at the woman as she tried to picture the creature. She had seen eagles before, but never a lion, so instead she pictured an eagle with the legs of a lizard, waddling around like the birds would.

"It looked upon our barren land, and at once, it took flight, its two wings splitting the earth. On one side, people with strong arms, colored hair, and normal faces were made. And on the other, a unique breed- people each with their own gifts and whims."

"Some had hair of purple and white, or others arms too short, but legs as tall as trees. Some couldn't work at all, but would smile at you and send you on your way."

"I've never met anyone like that." One of the children called out, hands curling to pout as the woman scanned the crowd, her eyes on Alyx. She reached out, grabbing her small hand and gently pulling her forward.

"Really? Not even someone like this young girl? Say little one, what's your name?"

Alyx found herself unable to speak when faced with the larger woman, staring at her with her big red eyes as she wondered how to reply. Mother had always told her not to speak with strangers, but she lit up from the compliment. She was special? How?

At last, she folded out, mewling out her name. "Alyx."

"Well, Alyx. You may not have brown hair, or brown eyes, but I can see the fire inside you. I can tell that someday, you're going to make something far bigger than yourself."

She didn't understand the full meaning of the woman's words, but smiled either way. Nobody had ever told her that, and she wondered what the fire in her was. Was it hot, and mean, like most other fires that she had met?

"Hey! Break it up, break it up!" A voice boomed, connected to a large figure who stomped through the crowd of children, wails following as they dived out of the way. A badge was on his chest, and he wore a hat.

"What do you think you're doing? You're holding up the entire road with your story! And poisoning our children it seems."

The woman held up her chin in response, a scowl forming on her face, unfazed by the larger man. "There's no law saying I can't tell a story to a few children, mayor."

Mayor? Alyx had heard the word before, and she knew he was important. But as she backed away from the hulking man, her small form shook, a new emotion filling her. She didn't want to leave the woman, but she also didn't want to stay there.

"There is when you hold up the entire road for it!" His vision snapped to the side, and when he saw Alyx, his face grew red, his fists curling even more.

"Disgusting! What do you think you're doing, harboring one of them? This town has had enough of their kind!"

Alyx began to step back, but her feet hit the uneven concrete, and she fell, her basket going flying to the side.

"Look at it! It can't even carry a basket. God knows why it's even here."

The woman kept a firm gaze on the man, grabbing her small bucket and moving towards where Alyx fell. Alyx tried to pull herself back up, her nose crying as she did.

"You should go, honey. Where's your mother? At the shops?"

Alyx gave her a resolute look, something which overwhelmed her fear. She remembered her mothers instructions, and that was to find Mr. Porter. If she didn't, her mother would be upset.

"No! Not until this basket is full!"

The mayor let out an annoyed groan, and began to approach them, with the woman's head snapping around. In a quick move, she grabbed a coin out of her bucket, dropping it into Alyx's basket. "Take this, instead. Just go."

Alyx was enthralled by the shiny, gold coin in her basket, and as she saw the mayor's shadow fall upon her, she finally turned to run.

Her basket thrummed in her fingers as she stared at the coin, only daring one glance back to the scene. The woman was now standing, seemingly in a shouting match with the mayor, who seemed about ready to do something. Something Alyx didn't want to see.

So instead, she turned to her house, and could already hear her praise in her ears. "Oh, Alyx, you got a coin! I'm so proud of you dear. What more could I possibly want from a daughter?"

The sweet, yet fake, melody soothed her as she made her way back home.

Chapter 3

King Xaden

The king was wildly undressing his extravagant garments as he ran towards the chambers in which his wife had been sleeping. He was in the middle of a meeting when the castle healer had rushed in, and before he even got the first few words out, he was rushing down the hall, his heart pounding in his ears as he did.

Now his marble palace seemed to be nothing more than a taunting maze for him, its size expansive and unyielding. With each footstep, he thought about his wife, and if she was alright, begging the gods to somehow shorten the length of the castle.

His wife had not been responding well to the healer's treatments, and he had already been warned of the possibility. To have a child was a great thing, but not all women could handle it. He had dismissed his healer at the time, telling him that if any woman could, it would be his wife. But now, as he rushed right into the unknown, he wasn't so sure of those words himself.

As he approached the door to their bedroom, two guards and a whole gaggle of other people were flocking there. Nobles, healers, and even servants seemed to be trying to push their way in, with the guards struggling to keep all of them back at once. Normally, such a lack of manners would be harshly punished, but in the castle's current state, all manners were cast to the side.

"Move!" His thundering voice seemed to scare off most of the crowd, bolting out of the way to make room for the king, now in an angry state, rather than his usual charismatic calm. He unceremoniously shoved the doors open and was greeted with his head healer and a few others crowding around the side of the bed.

His wife was pale, and looked tiny now on the bed. At first, he assumed the worst, before he heard an incessant crying, and he froze up right away, his hands unsure of who to reach for first. The healer lurched up from the bed, "Sire! Why do I have wondrous news for you."

"Are they going to be alright?" Still, a fear for his family clouded his judgment, and now, he was sure that his family included more than his wife. Now, he would surely have a child.

"The queen proves to be weak from birth, but I believe she will live. That is hardly the most exciting news, however."

Behind him, two of the healers were holding small figures, the first one was weeping and throwing its hands up in the air, as if it was having a tantrum even at this early age. Meanwhile, the other one was sleeping in the arms of the healer while they suckled their thumb.

The king felt entranced as his gaze shifted to the first baby, whose face was too familiar for him. The straight, small nose, along with big eyes that seemed to shine as if stars had been placed in them. The child was a perfect reflection of his wife, and he felt transfixed to stare at them.

"The gender?"

The healer's face fell to look grim as he peered back at his wife, then to him. "Both girls, my lord." The news would have been tragic, to most. To have twins was a blessing of fate, but to have two girls, when one needs heirs? But when he looked at the face of his daughter, who was now cuddled up to his side, he couldn't bring himself to care.

The healer continued to rattle off information, and he only smiled more as the healer revealed which was firstborn.

Even before that, he already knew she had to be his heir. But as he stared at the mini version of his wife, any of his doubts faded. He moved to the side of his wife, and her eyes creaked open, her skin still pale and no longer as smooth as it once was. But like him, her eyes were soon also drawn to their new daughter.

Her finger ghosted over the newborn, who let out a content giggle. "She's…" His wife trailed off as if she couldn't find the words, but he already knew the right ones to finish her sentence.

"Perfect."

His wife let a smile take her lips, and nodded. "Yes. Perfect."

At that moment, the other child began to break out crying, and their trance was broken as the healer lifted the other girl to him. A wave of reluctance washed over him of giving his daughter to his wife instead, but he finally relented and took the girl from the healer. At once, all his hesitance flooded away as he stared down at the crying blob he was holding.

"Have you thought about names?"

His wife nodded and pointed to the girl she was holding, "Ariel. Like the star." Ariel, the star of the singer. A star that always desired attention, and so the great gods moved her so the entire world would see her first. A fitting name for a princess.

"You always were good with names, dear."

She chuckled, "Of course I am. I'm the queen, aren't I?"

He shook his head, "Oh stop it you. Brag to the nobles, not the princess!"

She smiled at first, but then her gaze drifted to the child he held instead, and a frown took her face as she looked back up to him, eyebrow raised. "What about her?"

"I thought you might have a name?" It was the wrong response, for her face soured and she gave him a glare. The same glare she had whenever he tried to overrule her, something which he found soon faded away in their marriage. "Nemona?"

She raised her eyebrow more, "Go on."

He shrugged, "It suits her." And in his mind, it did. While one of his daughters seemed to be a natural ruler, the other was quiet, and seemed not to have the temper or ferocity needed of a ruler. But after all, only one of them could be the heir, so perhaps it was for the best.

She seemed to accept that and nod, and he let his finger drape over Ariel this time, who shot up right away, flailing her little arms around as if protesting his touch. *My little spitfire, and future Queen of Evalkyr.*

Chapter 4

Mil

Today has been a very, very, bad day. Mil still tried to recount the events that had led to his punishment in his head, and he still couldn't make sense of them. He had done everything right, yet somehow, trouble still found him. Or maybe he didn't, and he was just deluding himself?

But what was worse, is who he had been assigned to deliver news to. The Purist herself of all people, who he was sure would gobble him alive as soon as she found out of his punishment. He didn't want to go, but what choice did he have?

He tried to not let his head fill with the many tales he had heard of her. Some told him she was an angel both in mouth and in person, but others rumored that if he dared to echo bad news, he would be the one to bear the punishment.

He had done everything he could think of to purify himself, to make sure his hair was set back and clean, that not a speck of dirt was on his garments, and to remember the phrase he had been taught. *Service is absolute, and purity is final.* There would be no room for an imperfect messenger with her. If he wasn't already that.

But, he wasn't sure even that would be enough. Not with the news that he was going to be delivering. He could have let the scroll hang low and out of his sight, avoiding having let his curiosity get the better of him with a peak. Even then, it wouldn't matter, the news would have to reach her ears somehow.

When the grand door finally came into view, he let himself pause and stare at it. It seemed like something that would fit in nothing less than a castle, but its size was not what drew his eye. Instead, it was the patterns, and the creatures adorned in ivory and gold on its threshold.

The griffin screeched proudly at the top, claws drawn as it eyed up the foreboding threat. A manticore, one of great stature, and even more fierce than the tales had led him to believe. It too had its teeth and claws drawn, but the fate of this battle was left to anyone's imagination.

Of course, Mil had heard of the great beasts of old, animals that were as fascinating as they were conflicting. From his village, the only whispers he would have heard of them were hushed warnings of fear that they may ever return. But, now, as a Purist, any talk like that would land you in the cellar for a day or two, or worse.

He let his finger snake over the manticore's claws, tracing each edge. It gave him a sense of calm, that, perhaps at some point a powerful, yet fair creature walked these lands. Nothing like the dogs or horses, but intelligent, and pure. Taking a last deep breath, he let that calm surge him forward and push into the door.

A creak followed, and the golden door surged open, letting him glance into the long hallway ahead. A red carpet adorned the path, with torchlights to aid him in the oddly dark corridors. He let his feet guide him as he stumbled along, hearing the door close behind him.

Nothing about the area around him served to settle his nerves. He looked at the old paintings on the walls, or the murals that had the stuffed bodies of creatures. Half of them, he hadn't ever seen, and they seemed just as fairytale as the manticore or griffin had been.

Soon enough, he decided he saw enough of the fangs of mangled beasts, so he let his eyes droop to the floor, studying the endless patterns on the rug, which yet again featured the same creatures from the door, and others as well.

And then, the next thing he knew he was falling onto the hard floor, the rug twirling up behind him as his feet stuck in the air. But, it was the incessant laughing that followed that brought him up and onto his feet, his face flushed as he realized who this was.

The Purist sat in front of him, settled on a chair, and let him get his first good look at her. A yellow robe wrapped around most of her body, and jewels and patterns surrounded everywhere it went. As for her face, a white mask covered all of it, having only the imprints of eyes and a hole for a mouth. It was so shadowed, though, that he could hardly see even her lips. Maybe she didn't have them.

"I don't think I was expecting a visitor." There was the second thing that caught him off guard, he had come in expecting a grizzled, old lady, she sounded as if she was only a bit older than him, if that. But the reality of the situation hit as soon as his eyes lingered on the whip located behind her.

"I'm here with a message, m-ma'am!" He tugged the scroll from his cloak, setting it on the desk as he moved to attention, keeping his posture as rigid as he could. She looked to the scroll, then up to him, and the mask's mouth carved from a neutral expression, to that of a smirk.

"What's your name, acolyte?" He let his teeth bite into his lip as he considered what he should do. Why was she asking about him? Was he in trouble? If he thought the prior punishments he received were bad, what was bound to happen now?

"Mil, ma'am, err, is there a reason for you to ask?" The words cringed as they came out of his mouth, and he braced himself for a hard smack, but it never came.

"Mil." She repeated, leaning back as if it was of some importance. "Do me a favor, read the scroll, wouldn't you?"

Surprise overtook him at the request, but his arms moved faster than his brain as he scooped up the scroll, almost tearing it as he flung it open. Despite this, the Purist seemed unfazed as she looked at him expectantly.

> *"My Lady, I bring only grim news from the field. Arbornail and Fieldmoor still push back against us, even after their defeat. I fear that Evalkyr may soon send more troops, and we can not fend off both the locals and the army. The plague runs deep in these parts, and every day I find more and more of them hidden, or even worse, walking the streets. Should this continue, the towns may once more fall to their hands. I beg for the lady to respond to this threat, and drive back such evils.*
>
> *Dearly,*
>
> *General Benjamin"*

He was horrified. He knew of General Benjamin and his many exploits, but to think he was being defeated in battle? How could that be possible?

Yet, as the last words fell on his tongue, he was sure he was to be met with anger. After all, the purists had fought dearly to claim the two towns, and if they were to fall so soon, it would all go to waste. But the Purist merely hummed, and drummed her fingers against her mask.

"Quite a predicament, isn't it, Mil?"

He didn't understand why she was asking him. He should have been dismissed to leave already. But, he couldn't risk offending her.

He nodded furiously, "Of course, my lady!" He surrendered the scroll to her desk, letting his arms droop as she rose from her chair, looking right at him.

"What shall be done, Mil?"

"Pardon?" Were his ears hearing correctly? The Purist, asking him, the messenger? Everyone had assured him this job would be simple. He would go in, then he would go out, they reassured him. Maybe his fears were correct though. This really would be his downfall.

"Are you hard of hearing? I am asking you for your thoughts. Surely you understand the gravity of this situation." The request felt like a bull had suddenly decided to sit on him, as he felt stress creep up his neck and into his face.

He tried to think back on every lesson he had taken there, and every tutor that had told him of the Purist ways, and how they dealt with plague. Words floated around him until finally, he came to one, and the one that the tutors always seemed to echo with a sense of dread. For it was a final measure, done only when the plague could not be healed.

"A cleansing!" He managed to say those words with some level of pride, and when he saw the Purist's head raise, he continued, "If we can't deal with the locals and the army, then we need to dig out the plague before it drives the locals any further."

Cleansings were a rare action for the Purists to partake in. They preferred to coerce the towns to give up their plague, rather than to sour relations. But, wasn't it their job to get rid of the plague? That should be the priority.

An ear to ear grin emerged on the mask as the Purist sat up, clapping her hands together. "I did not expect them to send such a shrewd acolyte to me. Consider me impressed, Mil. Few are willing to resort to such drastic measures." She nodded to herself as she turned around to the wall, letting her hands tangle together.

Mil knew that a cleansing would be hard. The plague would fight back, and blood would stain the roads. But it was needed for the village to thrive, and the Purists' praise made him shoot up.

"Though it pains one to do, when plague is too prominent, we must take more active measures. And the Purists have more than been exhausted here." At that, she swung back around, looking at him once more.

Mil nearly jumped back at the motion. Even though she had been praising him, he still was jittery around her. What if she changed her mind? He couldn't let that happen.

"Tell your tutors that you are to return here tomorrow, by my orders. I would like to hear more of the ideas swirling around in that head of yours." Mil's eyes nearly bulged out of his skull when he processed what was being told to him. The Purist was requesting him to… rack his brain?

All his immediate worries fled him as he realized he wasn't going to be punished. Yet, new ones filled him. What could this possibly mean? Why would she be doing this?

He was left there, as still as a statue before her voice raised, "Now go, Mil, I'm sure you have many other duties to get to." He didn't need to be asked twice, and as he darted back down the hallway, he kept having the same question replay in his head. What in the name of all the lords just happened to him?

But as his footsteps rang away, the Purist once more turned to her back wall, and let her gaze wander to the sizable statue at her side. It was a griffin, and to the naked eye, it may have looked like any other ancient sculpture, but she knew better than that.

She let her hand rest on the statue's beak, and how easy it was then to picture the statue as a creature, moving in her room and speaking to her as any human may. "It will not be much longer, my friend. That, I promise."

Chapter 5

Benjamin

Benjamin scrunched his face up as his boots trudged through the muck below, the hollering of the plague and Purists alike leaving him with little to work with. The cleansing was meant to be a clean one, but the locals had proven to put up more of a fight than expected. The town was more plague-ridden than anything else he had seen, and the disgust that filled him was almost too much to shrug down.

He had lived to see the rise of the plague, and all the damage they could inflict. He had walked through the dead towns, where fair men would labor all day and night, while they sat and watched. He had seen how they turned fingers against one another, selling each other out for even the slightest crumb of bread. And yet, never had he seen a town so complacent to their ways, allowing the lame to order the strong, and perverting the natural order in a way too crude.

But soon enough, the plague would come to regret their many crimes, and he was proud to be at the forefront of it. "On my command!" His disciples took arms beside him, drawing their swords as they turned to him. He smirked as doors began to open, and the locals walked out, freezing in place as they looked at the force in front of them.

"Now." His disciples charged, and together, they were a force of fury. Doors flung open wildly as they charged in, and it was soon followed by a chorus of shouts, cracks, and breaks, and the houses were flooded only minutes after the siege began.

He waited as the minutes clicked by, and one by one, his disciples emerged from their homes, dragging struggling forms behind as they approached him. His lip pulled back in disgust as he witnessed the plague they brought with them, looking at each of them one by one.

He stepped forward to the first in line, looking from his stoic Purist to the form under him. The man, if he could even be called that, was a ragged thing, an ugly scar cutting across his face as his hair fell and balded, leaving only wrinkly and deformed skin in its wake. The plague, in its finest form.

He let his gaze rise to the crowd of locals that had gathered behind his men, all too scared to approach in fear of what may befall their plague-ridden counterparts. Disgusting. "To say I'm disappointed, would be an understatement. The purists have been nothing but generous to your town, giving you food, supplies, and water- and how do you repay us? By hosting the very plague that nearly drove your town to extinction in the first place!"

At that proclamation, he reached for the blade at his side, and let it slide away from its scabbard. By the time the plague realized what was to befall it, its eyes wide and its weak form struggling, it was already far too late for it. He let a sense of pride fill him as the blade met its target, and the plague slumped down, dropping as his disciple let his grip slip.

"The purists will not be taken advantage of! If you insist on both taking our resources and assisting the plague, we will have to drive it from your ranks!" He turned to nod to his disciples, and with that, the process began. He relished in the screams of the plague, and the eyes of the locals as they realized the gravity of the situation.

When the last of the plague fell to the floor below, his disciples moved beside him, and his eyes bore into those of the townspeople. "So then, what will it be? Can I trust that all future plague may be dealt with accordingly?" His only answer was sobs and wails as some locals, or the brave ones, dashed to the bodies below, and to him, that was an answer enough.

"Clear out the surrounding areas. I don't need any more of these plagueborn infecting this town." His disciples obliged, as they always did, and he was left to bask in the glow of victory. He had been concerned at first that the cleansing may just motivate the locals to rebel further, but it had the complete opposite effect.

He supposed that was his surprise for doubting himself to begin with, and even with all the plague around him, he let a smile come to his lips at that. Even now, after years of service, he still let his worries get the best of him, but it was no matter. He was correct, as he always was.

But as he let his eyes lazily wander the horizon, they snapped to a figure at the side. Under one of the houses, he swore he could see a white blob of sorts. He swung around, trying to get a better look, but as soon as he did, it jerked backward, moving under the house once more.

—

ALYX

Alyx had curled herself into a ball, covering her head with her arms as tears dripped from her face uncontrollably. Everything had happened in the blink of an eye, and she had run to the nearest place. Her house.

She broke through the door as soon as she reached it, but her mother wasn't anywhere. She jumped up the windows and tried to peek out, but her heart dropped at what she saw.

Everyone she knew was gathered up into the line, and cloaked figures surrounded them. Mr. Porter was there, and even that nasty mayor she had met only a few days prior.

But the two people that weren't there, who she wanted to run and cry to, were the storyteller she had met, and her mother. They were both strangely absent from the gathering.

Alyx already felt like she wanted to sink into the ground, trying to keep her sniffling down and her tears controlled. But that was before the real horror started.

She watched as a man approached Mr. Porter, observing his scarred face, and then, he pulled out his blade. She watched as a red liquid emerged from his throat, and his eyes seemed to crack as he crumpled to the ground.

But that wasn't the only thing she felt cracking as she watched. She felt something inside her, too.

She was frozen as they went down the line, continuing their practice to the rest of the people. Some they would pass, but others would soon be crumpling to the ground, just like Mr. Porter.

Panic consumed her all at once. She spun around and ran to the back of the house, hands searching the floor. Mothers voice sounded in her head, *"Alyx. Find the hatch. You'll be safe there."*

Her tiny hands grasped the trapdoor, and her arms ached as she pulled it up. It only creaked up a little bit, but it was all she needed. She squeezed through, ducking down so as to not hit her head.

She had never used the hatch before, and she started to look around. Darkness surrounded her, but she could still see light shining through the cracks. Her hand brushed against the dirt beneath her, and it hit her all at once. She was under the house.

She may have been safe, but she held her breath as she looked ahead. She was too scared to move, but she could still hear everything. Screams sounded out as people began to hit the floor, and Alyx could only see the boots of their attackers.

After at least a dozen bodies had hit the ground, the rest of the townsfolk broke down, while others remained silent, not moving an inch.

It was only then that Alyx dared to move, before stopping again. Two pairs of eyes watched her from the front, and she had to hold in a scream, wriggling back as far as she could. She had been spotted.

—

BENJAMIN

"Men!" At his call, two disciples emerged from the left, standing rigid as he pointed to the house. His gut told him that whatever that thing was, it certainly wasn't a normal critter, and he wasn't risking letting yet another plagueborn escape. Not this time.

"Stand at this side, and at my order, scare whatever is under it out. I will retrieve the creature once it emerges." Before waiting for acknowledgement from his men, he was already marching to the other side of the house, a new wave of determination coming upon him. Perhaps he had starved himself of the chase a bit too long, after all, he couldn't even recall the last time he got his hands dirty.

As he crouched down to look beneath the house, darkness seemed to obscure everything, until his eyes flashed to meet another pair. "You." He huffed, and shot his arm forward, trying to grab the scruff of whatever it was, though he missed.

The creature lunged out from under the house, starting on four legs, but then moving up to two as it bolted for the tree-line. It was then that he realized it wasn't a creature at all, but a human. She looked no older than five, and was dirtied beyond belief, her completely white hair specked with dirt and dust. She seemed more animal than human, and her skin was unnaturally pale.

"Plague." Understanding hit him like a bull, and he broke into a sprint after the being bolted for the tree line. He sprinted like there was no tomorrow, but the plague had a head start on him. It was already halfway to the treeline.

"Disciples!" He gritted his teeth as the blob hopped under a bundle of foliage, and after one pause, disappeared into the forest as a whole. He came to a sudden stop, not wanting to be swallowed by the forest before his men rejoined him.

"Master!" He heard the voice sound behind him, and his fingers tightened to fists. They both froze up at the sight, hobbling back a few steps. They went rigid when he yelled, however.

"You fools!" He spun around, his voice irate, as if it was on fire. Their masks slipped from the sound of it alone, and they went to put as much distance between them and their master as they could. "Tell me, what exactly took you so long to get here after I called for you? To the point a plagueborn could outrun you?!"

They had no answers, of course they didn't. Sometimes he forgot that incompetence ran in his ranks as well, and discipline must be dealt out as needed. Weak purists had no place in his ranks.

"You two are to report to your commanding officer and tell him of your folly. Am I understood?"

The two nodded, though he had a hunch they were doing so not out of regret, but out of fear of him. Pitiful, truly. He was about to send them off, before one spoke up. "Should we pursue the plagueborn, sir?"

His eyebrow raised at the disciple's eagerness to speak out so soon after being scolded. Perhaps one of them had a redeeming trait. "No. That beast won't last a day out in the woods, and I'm not wasting troops to pursue it. Consider it another tally in the cleansing."

As he turned back to face the woods however, he finally let his rage shine in his mind. A child not only outran him, but humiliated him in front of his men! And worse, it was a plagueborn child to boot. He could not be made to look a fool in front of his men. And with new resolve, he looked to the spot the plagueborn vanished to.

This would be the last time any plagueborn lived to see his face, and tell the tale.

CHAPTER 6

4 YEARS LATER

ARIEL

Ariel galloped around the bed, clutching her wooden horse as a tumbling fury chased her. She dodged to the side, before leaping up on the bed, scurrying across to her mothers side. Nemona followed, and she cuddled into her mother, hoping for some protection from the retribution that was to come.

Nemona let out a giggle, crawling over as she tried to grab the horse, and their mother didn't react, smiling at the two. Ariel was left trying to wrestle with Nemona, who proved to have a far stronger grip than she. She had to use every fiber of her being to keep her grip on, but she refused to let it go.

"Girls, girls. Come now, you can share the toy." Her mother reached down, grabbing the toy and laying it on the bed. "Why don't you play something together? I would have loved to have a playmate when I was your age."

Ariel snorted, "Like what?" She liked her sister, but the idea of having to give up her toy irked her. She wanted to keep running around the bed like a horsey, not give it to Nemona!

"Well, when I was a child, I liked to play princess and prince. One of you will be the valiant prince, and the other will be the damsel princess."

Ariel puffed her chest up, "I'll be the prince!" She didn't wait for a reply from Nemona, and hopped down from the bed, raising her toy horse high.

"Princess, your savior is here!" She exclaimed, watching with a smile as Nemona stared at her for a few moments, before shambling off without the toy.

She threw her arms up, falling down as fake tears fell from her eyes. "Help! Help!" She cried, as if she was a real damsel in distress.

Ariel was thrown out of her playful mood for a moment, but went right back into it. Grabbing her horse, she hit the first figure she could see, an ugly looking knight. The wooden toy crashed to the ground immediately. "Take that!"

She threw her arms to her hips, making a heroic pose. In her mind, she pictured squires and kings all standing in a row, singing their praises to her as she feasted on as much candy and meat as she could.

Nemona was left lying on the ground, staring at the ceiling as she waited for a reply. She didn't call out to Ariel or ask her to keep going, but laid firm into the ground. At that, their mother finally stirred up, her attention drawn from her task.

"Now, girls." Ariel didn't respond to her, which caused her mother to sigh, and in a sterner voice she said, "Ariel!"

Ariel turned to her mother, dropping her horse toy as she tried to evaluate the scene. She knew her mother was using the 'trouble' voice, but she couldn't tell why. She was doing what she wanted, after all.

"You need to include Nemona when you're playing. What is the valiant princess without her knight, after all?"

Ariel tried to consider this reasoning, imagining a large X being drawn through her father and mother. She saw their sad faces as they were pulled apart, and it clicked in her mind. Were Nemona and her the same? That X was a bad thing between them?

Her mothers face softened, and she patted the bed. "Come here you two. I'll tell you both a story." They didn't need another word, and raced up to get on the bed, jumping with joy. Their mother had many stories, and each was just as exciting as the last.

"When I met your father, he was just like you Ariel. We both wanted to make things work, but everything had to be his way. Walks in the garden, meals, even what room we stayed in, and well…"

Her mother trailed off, a sheepish look on her face as she stuttered. "Our playtime. It had to be his way." Ariel didn't know they also played horse, but it made her excited! Maybe they could all play together one time. Father was always so busy.

"But he wanted to make things work, and in the end, we were inseparable. He still kept some of his wants, but he included me, and wasn't so hung up on every little detail." She touched both of their noses, chuckling as Ariel reared up, touching her nose in response.

"We were just like you two. You both are inseparable, but you're being drawn apart by small differences. You're sisters, and you'll need each other-."

Mother was interrupted when she broke into a coughing fit, falling back on the bed. Ariel went to her side, pushing at her shoulder, but it didn't seem to rouse her. Nemona came behind her, peering over her with bulging eyes.

Their mother tried to straighten herself, but the coughing kept coming. A smile broke onto her face nonetheless as she tried to hide her coughs. "Ariel. Go get the maids. Hurry!"

She wasn't sure what happened next, but she turned and hightailed it out of the room at once. The maids were waiting right outside, and they had taken off before she even finished her sentence.

"Ariel!" Nemona called out, and Ariel shot around back to the room. Nemona was sniffling, and no matter how much they screamed, mother didn't answer them.

Nemona wrapped Ariel up in a hug, and pulled her aside. Finally, Nemona got her words out between tears, "Castle. I want to go to the castle."

Ariel perked up at the idea. Whenever Nemona and her went there, everything seemed to fix itself. Eventually, mother would come and scold them for sneaking off.

The two girls got on all fours, squeezing their way under the bed. It was completely dark down there, and Ariel couldn't hear any coughing. She was about to say something to Nemona, before heavy footsteps entered the room.

Ariel saw at least four pairs of feet, and a familiar voice spoke up. It was her father. He let out a cry, and ran beside the bed. A few thumps followed from above, and another voice spoke up.

"Sire. We must move her to the infirmary at once. Her pulse is faint."

Father didn't argue as two of the maids stepped forth, and lifted mother off the bed. Ariel held her breath, staring back at Nemona.

Father exited soon after, and the healer followed behind him. They were all alone, and Ariel let out a cry. Why did they take mother away? What was father doing?

Nemona patted her on the back. "Don't worry, Ariel. Mother is just tired."

The answer seemed so easy to Ariel. Of course mother was fine. She was just sleeping, and father couldn't wake her.

Nemona hugged her again, and Ariel snuggled into the embrace. She turned to Nemona. "You promise, Nemona? Mother's going to be alright?"

Nemona sniffled, but nodded. "I promise."

Ariel smiled, and let her body relax. Everything was going to be alright.

—

The next few months passed like a whirlwind, and Ariel could only recall parts of it. She no longer got to visit her mother, even when she got on her knees and begged the maids to. Instead, she was dismissed and told to go back to playtime.

Nemona didn't say anything about it, but Ariel felt like she also could tell something was up. She didn't have an interest in playing much anymore, so they would sit around the table drawing instead.

One night, she snuck out of her room and hoisted herself up onto a chair, peering into the room she used to be with her mother in. She saw an empty room, with a frozen figure in the bed. She tried to open the door, but the lock wouldn't budge.

She was strictly monitored when she was found, and she wasn't able to find her way back to the room again. For now, her memories of playtime were in the past, and she was only left with her juvenile thoughts to contend.

Eventually, they were interrupted when a group of maids in black came to greet them. They didn't say a word to them, even as they were barraged with questions, and instead escorted them out into the courtyard.

A huge crowd of people were there, and the maids escorted them to the side, then up a long row of staircases. They did not join them, but insisted they go up. Ariel felt her legs ache as she took the first few steps, her head turned to the side.

Everyone watched as they ascended, Ariel leading the charge. Their father was at the very top of the case, and in front of him lay a big block of cinder. Ariel hopped to the top, deciding she didn't like the big crowd.

Their father rested his head on the case, and as Ariel came to the top, she could see what was inside it. A large glass pane rested on the top, and inside, she could see her mother, sleeping. Why had father put her in a box? And why was everyone there?

"Why is mom in there, dad?" Nemona came hurtling up behind her, but she didn't glance inside the box. Instead, she slouched down, huddling in the corner. She didn't dare to ask the same question Ariel had.

"Girls." He paused, wondering how to break this to the two. "You won't be able to play with your mother anymore. She's taking a trip to a place, far, far away from here."

Ariel felt a tear drip down her face, and let out a wail. She wouldn't get to play with mother anymore? Why? Her wails multiplied, and soon enough the crowd was turning to face her as tears flowed from her like a river.

Her father nodded to the maids, "Take them back to their room." Ariel wasn't able to get another word out before she was whisked away and back down the steps, watching as her father grew fainter and fainter.

He opened his mouth, a bellow of words pouring out, but she couldn't make them out, far too preoccupied with her own sadness.

—

Ariel didn't know how long it was, until at last, her father returned to the room her and Nemona shared. He didn't have the usual joy that touched his face, but instead, an edge was plastered over all of him.

"Ariel, come with me."

She didn't want to leave Nemona, but with his tone, it didn't take much for her to scurry along to his side. She gave a passing glance to her sister, before the door shut behind her, and she was being led down the halls.

At last, they came to a giant bedroom, which he led her into. A beautiful bed adorned the center, with all sorts of furniture around it. It was something only fit for royalty, and was far more extravagant than the nursery she was in.

"This is your new room, Ariel. The maids will move your items in by tonight."

Ariel cocked her head, surveying the room, but found a key piece missing. She turned back to her father, trying to read his expression, but failed to.

"What about Nemona?"

He shook his head. "Ariel, you're the heir of this country. Because of that, certain duties are expected of you. I wanted to wait longer, but now I can't. Your formal education will begin today, and there can't be any distractions."

Ariel didn't understand what was being told to her, and she shot around. She bolted out of the doorway, running towards the one room she knew, her nursery.

She heard her fathers voice behind her, but perhaps he was far too worn out to catch her. Her legs stung, but she made it to her destination nonetheless.

But when she opened the door, she didn't see Nemona, or any of their items. Instead the room was filled with maids, all of whom were throwing books and toys alike into boxes. Three of them were trying to break down the bed, and Ariel let out a cry. "Stop! Put those down!"

They all paused, murmuring quiet words to one another before a heavy-set maid stepped up to her. "Princess, you're getting older. You now need to focus on princes and fashion, not children's toys."

She let out another wail as she remembered herself playing with Nemona, her mother watching from above. "No! They're mine!"

The heavy-set maid pulled back, putting a hand on Ariel's shoulder but not saying anything more. Everyone froze though when crushing footsteps made their way to the door.

Her father was now in the doorway, looking down at the maid with a frown, before turning to look at Ariel. He levied a look to her that made her freeze, and she looked back to the room. The heavy-set maid had already retreated, as if she had never talked to Ariel to begin with.

Why had everything gone so wrong on that one day?

CHAPTER 7

4 YEARS LATER

NEMONA

Rain poured down from above as Nemona trudged on, not sure of where she was going. She had resolved to keep walking, even as her shoes got mucky, and rattled against the concrete. Her hood barely protected her from the weather, and most other people in the streets had already cleared out.

It all happened over one small disagreement. She had seen Ariel every other day or so in the garden. With nobody watching, they could still play like they were kids. But once the maids learned what they were doing, everything changed.

It took only a few weeks before she caved, and she demanded to see Ariel again. The maids scolded her for acting so childishly, and lectured her on the queenly duties Ariel had to do. Nemona cried the more she heard.

She knew she should have kept quiet and accepted it was going to happen, but she felt something in her break at her toys being taken away. They were the only memory she had left of a time when things were different, but she knew why they were being taken. That time was long gone.

But now she was facing the consequences of her actions, and she was stuck in the town. She knew night was already upon her, and that the streets grew rougher as soon as the sun set. She had heard stories from the maids about how terrifying the world outside was, and how the people of Evalkyr would eat up a young, defenseless girl.

The only thing that stood out among the gloomy keep was a torch-lit building, with a man calling out to anyone that passed by. He seemed to be middle aged, with a black, well-shaven beard and hair that matched. He wore a red cloak, and when he saw her, he couldn't look away.

Nemona was ready to bolt, but instead he lowered himself to the ground, beckoning her closer. "What are you doing out here, girl? Are your parents nearby?"

Nemona hadn't seen her mother in years, and now, the truth had started to sink into her as she realized she may never again. And she had a feeling her father was probably busy with his own matters. He only ever visited her when Ariel was around, after all.

She shook her head to the question, hanging her body low as her frown only grew. She didn't want to be reminded of all the sad things going on. She wanted to have something bright and happy.

"You shouldn't be out here alone. Come inside." He motioned his hand, moving the curtain so she could see inside. Bright lights were everywhere, and people were sitting around tables dealing cards to one another. A warm energy flooded out, and before she knew it, her legs were carrying her in.

There weren't any other children in there, and the chatter of adults filled her ears. She turned, not sure what way was the right direction, and instead resolved to follow her guide. "Do your parents live in the slums? High town? First Circle?" He rattled off names, but she kept her head down, not answering.

When he saw that she wasn't going to respond to him, he moved the both of them towards a round table near the back. On it, a farmer sat on one side, playing against what she could only assume was the embodiment of what the maids scorned.

"Hey, boys. We have a newcomer."

They both turned to look at her, eying her up like she was an oddity. "Ain't she a little young to be playing? Poor thing probably doesn't have a buck to even bet." It was true. She didn't have any money on her, but the fact she would have to was concerning her.

"She doesn't have to worry about it. I'll bet for her." He pulled a few coins out of his pocket, placing them on the table below. "She can go against the loser of you two." They turned to smirk at each other, as the farmer put down a purple stone into a board in front of him.

She leaned up, trying to understand the board in front of her. Six holes were lined up on either side, and the stones were being put into them. The farmer had two stones in his, while the other had five.

Her guide cut in, "The aim of the game is to get all holes filled with pebbles. But, you can only fill one if you get a winning card." He nodded to the stack of cards each of them had, which were now drawn out as they flipped through them.

"Oh, I got a good set! You better be scared now." The farmer laughed, placing a card face down. The more dirty looking man smirked, and placed one down as well. When both of them drew their cards, the farmers had a star, and the others a sun.

"Sun beats star, mate."

The farmer let out a wail as he stared at the two cards, shocked at how he could lose his gamble. The dirty man laughed as he took the coins placed on the table, shoving them into a bag he held close. Nemona watched like a hawk, trying to wrap her head around the intricacies.

Her guide spilled a wad of coins onto the table, and nodded for Nemona to take the now vacant seat to his right. She managed to pull herself up, and was staring right into the face of the farmer. He grumbled, but his grumble stopped when he laid eyes on the coins.

"Introduce yourself to the girl, Tom. I'll go get some drinks for you two."

Tom, as he was called, let out a groan as he pulled the stones out, reshuffling the decks of cards. "What do ye need to know, hun?" His voice was soft, but Nemona felt something familiar ooze off it. It was the same voice her father would use, the last times she saw him.

"Your family?" Was he like her father, in more than just his tone? Did he have children like them, and a wife that had been carted off? She tried to imagine the picture of her family, and then another right next to it. She was only living a normal life, she supposed.

"I got a son. He's a good man, but I ain't doing much for him. No wife, no family, just us two. Life never gave us many favors."

Nemona nodded her head, putting her finger to her chin as she tried to pick apart the words she was being given. 'Life never gave us many favors' was something she didn't fully understand, but she felt it strongly.

At that, the guide came back, two large jugs on his tray. He handed one to Tom, and then one to her. She stared at the murky brown liquid, bringing it back to take a gulp. As soon as the bitter stuff hit her tongue though, she pushed the jug onto the table, coughing it up.

The two men let out a hearty laugh, and Tom grabbed her jug for himself. "Now then, why don't we get started!"

Her guide came to her side, whispering a few words of advice into her ear. "Try to keep the strongest cards on your deck, and when you can't read him, put them down. When he seems confident, react, and when he seems weak, do the same. Got it?"

Nemona didn't nod this time, too transfixed with the cards in front of her.

The game was moving faster than she expected, and soon enough, she had managed to get four pebbles, and he got five. Sweat beaded down his forehead as he juggled his cards, staring at the coins neatly placed on the table.

He placed down a card, and Nemona could see it ever slightly. It was a river, which was a gamble. She looked to her deck, a clear lightning card in one, and a fire card in the other. A winning card, and a losing card.

The coins didn't grab her eye, and she could feel the energy that radiated off the man. It hit so close to home, and it made her want to talk to him more. To ask him why, what his relationship with his son was, and more.

She grabbed her fire card, and placed it down on the table, looking at him as she waited for the cards to be drawn. A few moments passed, and he drew up the cards, staring at his river and her fire.

He threw his hands up, letting out a cheer as he grabbed his sack, pushing all of the coins into it. His body danced without permission, his muscles twitching about ready to burst. "Did you see that, Dylan? Good luck is finally favoring me!"

This Dylan turned to look at her, his brows furrowing as he stared at the lightning card she still had in her deck. He didn't speak, until at last, his face rose, and he flashed her a smile and a nod.

"Well, guess you are a lucky one, Tom. Spend the coins wisely, won't you?"

Tom snorted, insulted by the suggestion he may not. "These girls here," He patted his sack, "Are my babies, I won't be parting from them for a good while."

The two bantered back and forth for a bit longer, and Nemona let a grin engulf her face. She hadn't had this much fun in a while, and even now she could feel warmth seep into her. But then again, her head drifted to the door, which she swore she could almost see the castle from.

Dylan turned to her at last, looking to the door with her. "Will you finally tell us where your parents are, hun? I'm sure we can point you in the right direction."

Nemona looked back at the pub, and hesitated, but let her cooler self prevail. She trotted over to the door, pointing out its windowed panes to a building ahead. It was the castle, and it towered over everything else around it.

Dylan's jaw dropped, and he looked back to the unkempt clothing she wore. "A servant girl? You really shouldn't be out here alone. Are your parents back at the castle?"

She nodded, and he pointed to a back way that cut in between two large buildings. "Take that path, and once you hit the main road, turn right. If anyone approaches you that you don't know, run the other way, alright?"

Nemona felt a shiver go through her at the thought of who may be approaching her at that hour, and she imagined they wouldn't be as charitable as Dylan.

She turned to give a passing wave to Tom, who smiled and waved back at her as he jiggled his sack at her, chuckling. A toothy grin broke out on her face as she turned, walking out the door. She looked back, getting a final look at Dylan as he slinked away, before waddling to the path he had pointed out.

The castle loomed over her, almost tauntingly so, and its shadow was hardly as warm. The cold air brushed against her exposed skin, and she pulled her cloak up, praying to arrive soon.

—

When she found her way to the castle, she had to crawl back in through her tunnel, arriving at a very plain looking hall. Nobody was running around, and she did not get any sight of her maids. Instead, it looked like the castle always did at night, quiet and eerie.

She found her way back to her room, and opened the door, looking at the dark expanse in front of her. The candles had been blown out, but she could still make out the room in front of her. Her toys had been stripped away, and the room was now devoid of all color.

It was plain, and the small bed and dresser were the only pieces that stood out, apart from the bright and bland rug that covered the floor. Nothing about the room screamed to her, and worse, none of her maids were there either. They all were gone.

She stared at it for a few more seconds, before shutting the door, not daring to look back. She could hear voices down the hall, and at once recognized it to be her maids.

"And then the girl went and blimey ran off! I swear, those who deal with the Crown Princess don't have to put up with this. Who knows where she even went off to."

Another cut in, "What about the guards? Didn't you tell them?"

"What's the point? She'll come crawling back sooner or later, no need to mobilize a castle wide search. The king is far too busy to bother himself anyway."

Nemona felt the words pierce her, and not wanting to face the maids, she turned, running in the other direction. She knew what they said was true, but to hear it out loud, and so clearly?

She should have known better to expect anything else, she supposed. She had deluded her mind too much to see the truth that was right in front of her.

She made her way to a spare bedroom, bland, yet still with more color and accessory than her own room. A painting was held high on the wall, and she stared at the art of a swan that was plastered on it. A breeze floated in from the window, and she turned to its open form.

She gave one last look to the lights below, where the town was now coming alive, with a few groups marching up and down the streets. To her, they were only specks in the distance, but she had to wonder if one of them was Tom or Dylan.

With one final look, she pushed the window shut, closing out any view she may have of the world below. She turned to her bed, and resigned herself to a sleepless and restless night.

PART 2: THE SICKLY SEED

CHAPTER 8

1014 AD

ANITA

Anita let her footsteps creak through the hallway, her eyes caught on the door ahead. She gave a passing glance to the blockade she had stepped over, glee filling her. Whatever was going on there, they didn't want her to see, and that made it even better.

She could hear loud voices splitting through the room, and let her hands rest upon the door separating her from them. She pulled it open, letting only a creak show, and glanced into the giant room it hid.

The room itself was not extraordinary, with its only odd feature being a pool in the middle of it. But around it, The Purist and her commanders were gathered, as well as a few other figures. And at the rear, a giant statue was placed on a wagon. *A griffin?*

Taking in a deep breath, she pushed herself against the door. It gave her a good enough view of the room, and even she wasn't reckless enough to waltz in.

Three Purists panted as they pulled it forward, dropping it just before the pool. The Purist gave an intent look to Benjamin, beckoning him forward with a wave of her arms.

Benjamin had a long smirk covering his face, and at once, he started to remove his shirt. The buckles went, then the cloak, and at last, he was shirtless in front of everyone. Anita cringed at the gesture, Purists were meant to be covered up, after all. *But that only made it more interesting.*

"Commander Benjamin has gone above and beyond in his time as a general. From my counts, he has exterminated close to a thousand plague, and saved two towns from the reaches of our neighbor."

Muted cheering broke out among the spectators, but Anita could tell it was faint. Nobody there was too interested in the commander's feats, clearly.

"I have not seen such talent since the formation of the purists, and as such, I had no choice but to promote him to Commander." The Purist gave a nod to a woman in the crowd, who Anita recognized at once.

Commander Trisha was there, which meant every commander was as well. What was so important that The Purist called home all of her highly ranking Purists?

Trisha stepped forward, a golden necklace in her hands, that she dropped onto Benjamin's neck. The two held a stare for a while, until at last, Benjamin looked away. Anita let out a small chuckle, what a pushover.

At that, the Purist turned to the statue, and placed her hands upon it. Nothing happened at first, until something hit Anita right in the chest. She toppled over, only just catching herself by her hands. *Maybe my luck finally has ended.*

But when nobody came to check on her, she dragged herself up and peaked into the room.

Her eyes widened as she watched, for everyone else had been knocked over as well, except the Purist and Trisha. A bright yellow light flooded out from the Purists' hands, and she once more hit the statue.

A crack formed in it, then another, as chunks of the stone began to fall off. Instead of leaving holes, however, white feathers were left in its place.

The stone continued to fall off, until one leg, an eye, and some of the body were left exposed to the world. The eye snapped to the Purist, and the creature's claw lunged out, trying to slash at her robes.

The Purist leapt back, narrowly missing the blow. The creature's maw was still covered in stone, but it's pupil slit as it tried to writhe to freedom. The Purist seemed unfazed, and lifted her hands once more.

The same energy of before flooded out of the creature, and right into the Purists hands, only causing the beast to struggle more. She turned her attention to Benjamin, and the energy flooded from her fingertips, right into the necklace Benjamin wore.

"Now!"

Her voice boomed across the room, and Benjamin obliged, sinking into the waters below until his head was under. A second passed, then another, and soon enough Anita swore it had been a whole minute.

Hair rose, and then a face, and his entire body came up, but different than before. He no longer had the wrinkles of a middle-aged man, and instead, had the face of a young one.

"Try to remove the necklace." The mask on the Purists face twisted upward, forming a smile. Anita's eyes widened, as the Purist never smiled. Nothing about this situation was normal.

Benjamin let out a huff, but did try to tug the necklace off, to no avail. The metal was stuck to his neck, and no amount of pulling dragged it off.

"Excellent." The Purist turned to the statue, who continued to glare daggers at the both of them. "You may return to your slumber now, Purity. Your services are no longer required."

The beast lunged out its claw again, but it was to no avail, as stone began to retake the living parts. As its body began to cover up, it tried to slash at the Purist again, but she was too far for it to reach.

It struggled much like a dying bug, and Anita wanted to scoff. For something that seemed so mythical, it acted no better than a cornered animal.

When the statue was whole, the Purist snapped her fingers, and three Purists emerged to drag it away. Another round of cheering broke out, and Anita pushed the door shut.

This was what the Purist didn't want anyone to see. She had a living statue, and was wielding what Anita could only describe as magic.

Anita gritted her teeth. She wanted to stay longer and watch, but time was running out. Jasper said she had left to retrieve his cloak. If she stayed here any longer, people would start to ask questions. She also would prefer to not have to charm any more guards on her way here.

How stupid they can be. So afraid of that disgusting plague, but this trusting of their own members? She had to stop herself from gagging at the picture of the plague. She had only ever met one before, and probably one of the worst.

When she bumped into him, he wouldn't stop saying thank you to her. A constant ring of please's came out as well, but that was all she needed to hear. No non-plague could be that stupid. She ran him through with her sword as soon as she could.

No, the purists were right about that. But that didn't mean she trusted them either. She almost started to believe they really were just do gooders, too oblivious to see their own faults. But this? No, the Purist knew what she was doing. And that, she could use.

She turned, tiptoeing out of the hallway and back to where she came. A plan was already forming in her mind, and she knew exactly how to use this information.

Chapter 9

Arnold

Arnold chittered his teeth as he approached the forest, clinging onto his dagger a bit too intently. The other two let out laughs as they watched him, with Duncan coming to slap him on the shoulder.

"Cheer up, mate. What's the worst that could happen?"

He already knew the answer to that. He had heard rumors of those who came into the woods and never came out, and the beasts that would drag them into their lairs. Only skeletons would remain of them.

The worst tale, though, was that of the Woodland Ghost. It was a blur of white they said, with demonic red eyes and teeth as sharp as nails. It spoke in a feminine voice, and would kill anyone that trespassed onto its land.

Some spoke of seeing it drag carcasses to its base, and of it covered in mud, eating like a wild animal. It would rip the meat off the animal it hunted, not daring to use forks or anything that even resembled humanity.

He wondered why he had accepted the deal Duncan and Gregory had presented him. It seemed gracious at first, to hunt whatever they could find and sell it for a mountain of gold back at Arbornail. But now, as he could hear the roars of the forest, he wondered where he went wrong.

Upon seeing him trail behind, Duncan let out another laugh. "What's scaring you Arnold? Afraid the Woodland Ghost is gonna come get you?" Gregory held his knees and let out a bellowing chuckle, pointing at Arnold.

When he didn't reply, their faces both paled. "You're actually scared of that story? Oh come on, Arnold. It isn't even real to begin with. The purists would have killed it if it was."

It was true that the purists usually dealt with creatures like that, but he wasn't so convinced. They must have missed this one, because the stories he heard were far too real to be fiction. "But what if it is here? It'll kill us all, and hang us for good measure!"

Gregory rolled his eyes, stomping up to him and grabbing his cloak to drag him along. "Oh stop with your constant worrying Arnold. We can never take you on adventures anymore. You'll be owing us an apology once we get back."

Arnold let out a gulp, but continued on, following the shadows of his two companions. Maybe they were right, and he was getting himself worked up over nothing. He took a deep breath, and let his mind clear of any worries.

A sudden rattle came out, and Arnold turned, yelling, "The Woodland Ghost!" The other two flung around, staring at an empty bush. It was silent for a moment, before they broke out laughing.

"Scared of wild animals already, Arnold? You'll need more confidence than that out here!"

Gregory and Duncan turned ahead, ignoring Arnold as he stared. After a minute, he turned to follow his companions, and as he did, a pair of eyes emerged from the bush. Bright red eyes.

—

ALYX

Alyx watched the three men walk through the territory, destroying anything that came in their path. They cut down trees and smashed the ground, making a hole wherever they went.

When they found a herd of deer, grazing in a field, the three split up, forming a ring formation around them. At once, arrows flew from all directions, landing into the deer.

The deer cried out, and split into different directions, kicking up ash as they did. Alyx reeled back into the foliage, furrowing her brows. When the dust cleared, at least six deer had been downed by the flurry of arrows.

Nobody needed that much to survive. They were hunting for mere sport. Her veins boiled at the thought, and she clawed at the nearest surface- tree bark. *Just like them. Exactly like them.*

The deers bodies lay still, the same as many others, and blood soaked out of them. She watched as the scene flashed away, and instead of deer, a pile of humans sat in the middle. Cloaked figures surrounded them, swords drawn as they laughed at the scene.

In unison, the laughter rang out within the two memories, and the three men stepped forward. "Look at that! Six pelts, that'll easily get us at least ten gold coins."

Another nodded, "And only a few arrows as well! These beasts are getting weaker by the day."

A call rang out from one of the deer, an arrow lodged in its leg as it tried to stand up, blood gushing out of the wound. Alyx wanted to speak to it, to tell it to play dead, but it was far too late.

One of the men spun around, slashing the creature's face with his dagger. The deer screamed louder as it tried to writhe away, but it was too injured to stand.

"Darn beast! Die already!"

The third man backed up to the bush where she was, hands raised as he shouted out something to the rest of the group. Alyx looked back to the bloody creature, and lunged.

She dragged her crude dagger out, slashing at the man's shoulder. He let out a childish wail, swinging around to face her, but far too late. Her dagger bounced up, right into his fleshy neck.

Blood spewed out, launching into her face and white hair, staining it a sickening hue. The man tried to grasp his throat, gagging as blood spilled out. Alyx smashed into him, knocking him down to the ground below.

The other two swung around, their expressions fading as they took in her blood covered self. "The Ghost!?" They moved away from the deer, and Alyx saw that it was still trying to stand. *A fighter. Just like her.*

"It can't be! It was just a myth!" The man's gaze flickered to the one she had killed, and his face dropped. "Arnold! Get up!" He yelled, but there was no movement from the body.

She approached them, her dagger in hand, not responding to any of their cries. She had heard too many of them already. For every step she took forward, they took back, their hands raised in surrender.

"We didn't mean anything, Ghost! We were just hunting our fair share. Ain't that right Gregory?" Pleading. Alyx hated it in her direction, and from such scum. Pleading was something only true victims deserved.

"Yeah! We didn't mean anything, we swear." When she didn't reply, this Gregory crept up, hands forward as if approaching a rabid dog. "We don't mean any harm. Now, if you could let us go-."

She jumped forward, digging her teeth into his fingers. He screamed, pulling his hand back and bolting away from her. He didn't stop at the canopy, and continued into it. "Gregory! Wait!"

The second one followed in suit, and she watched until they were consumed by the forest. They wouldn't make it a day out there without their tools.

But with them gone, her gaze turned to the deer, who still clung onto life. The others had long since perished, but it looked to her with big eyes, asking a question. *Will you kill me?*

Alyx could have. It would give her another meal for the day, but the more she stared into the deer's eyes, the more she paused. The deer was young, and a doe from what she could tell. It had a whole life ahead of it, and so far, it had survived life's challenges.

She leaned down, pulling the arrow out of its shoulder as it buckled away from her. The slash on its face and leg needed to be covered, or else it would grow infected. She remembered when she made the same mistake, and her hands grew purple and wretched.

She turned to the canopy around her, grabbing a vine off the hanging trees. She pulled it into a loop, tying it on one end and approaching the deer. She threw it over its neck, stringing it until it fit into a nice collar.

The deer stared at her, and she pulled forward, trying to get it to walk. After a begrudging moment, it pushed forward, getting to its legs, albeit with struggle. It wobbled as it stepped forward, freezing to look at Alyx.

Alyx returned the deers gaze, and at last, it walked forward, following her as she tugged it into the forest. No being deserved to suffer, and she would ensure this one's pain ended.

—

A week had passed since the men had intruded, and she had managed to string vines and leaves together to create a bandage over the deers wounds. It still wobbled as it walked, but she had tied it to a tree near her camp for now.

The flesh had started to grow and heal, and she could tell it would survive this, one way or another. But for now, she was more focused on the men. Anger flushed through her at the thought, and she wondered why she let them get away.

Because bad men always do. That's how the world works.

But if they came back, then what? She stared at the few supplies she had. She had looted a few coins off the man's body, and she had the meat and pelts from her previous kills. She knew what way they were going, south, towards the villages.

She had never wanted to go back, but now she may not have any choice. *Could she let them walk free, without punishment?*

She turned back to the deer, and the two had one of their long staring matches again. At last, she stepped forward, and brought the vine off the creature's neck. It gazed at her again, not moving as it shook its body out.

"Go on. You have a herd out there." *Unlike me.*

The deer let out a snort, and then took off, bounding into the forest and out of her camp. She likely would never see it again, but in her heart, she knew it would do well in life. Or, at least as well as she had.

But for now, she fixed her gaze south. Towns weren't like the forests. Bad men plagued them, and she wouldn't let that spill into her peaceful home.

CHAPTER 10

MIL

A good-sized crowd was packed below the stage, small compared to the entire temple, but large enough that Mil felt important. It was a rewards ceremony, and Mil had a feeling he was receiving one. He didn't know for what, but the Purist had been hinting at 'good omens' for months now.

The ceremony should have been beneath the Purist, but she had made an appearance regardless. She stood to the side, while a high ranking Purist stood at the front of a podium. Mil didn't know his name, but the etchings on his robe gave away his status.

Beside him was Bolios, his fists raised in celebration as he made no effort to hide his excitement. To his other side was General Monbek, who had an arm placed on his shoulder. The man had helped them get to this point, and he responded to the gesture with a half-smile.

The speaker read out a few names, giving out awards for various things, nobility, honor, most plague exterminated. The more and more names he heard, the more he rose on his toes, his ears jumping for a certain sound.

"General Monbek, please step forward."

His mentor creased his eyebrows, letting his hand glide from

Mil's shoulder as he marched up to the front of the room. The speaker continued, "Due to your intense dedication, a high honor has been bestowed upon you. You will serve as the head of the Talibuk Temple, after the passing of their head."

The Talibuk Temple? But that was all the way at the border. Would he and Bolios be moving there, instead? Would that mean he couldn't interact with the Purist anymore?

General Monbek let his jaw fall, eyes wide as he took in the news given to him. With a bow, he nodded, "Of course, Disciple Atticus. I am honored that you have granted me with su-."

Before he could finish his statement, the disciple cut him off, "Yes, yes, now move along please. We have many more honors to get to."

The two shared a short look before Monbek returned, shaking his head at Mil. Mil was appalled by the rudeness of the man. This was an important honors ceremony, and he was treating it like nothing. *But the Purist wasn't doing anything about it. Maybe Monbek shouldn't have spoken up?*

The speaker looked down to the scroll he was reading, and he stopped speaking, his head snapping to the Purist. She looked at him just as intently, and he went back to reading right away.

"As he will be away, his apprentice, Mil, shall be named a General in his absence. Mil, you have impressed us all with your performance in regards to Fieldmoor and Arbornail. Your quick thinking has saved many of our soldiers' lives, and so, let me bestow you this honor. You may now name your second."

Mil froze up, his mind racing with different thoughts. *A general? He would be the same rank his mentor was?* He suddenly didn't feel as ready as before, and his body shrunk. It was true that he had been a great help in securing the two rogue towns, but his training still only started two years ago.

With a large amount of beading eyes on him, he wobbled forward. There was only one clear choice for his second, Bolios. He was his closest ally, and the only one he could trust. "I choose Bolios as my second, sir."

The man surveyed Bolios, and snapped his lips together. *Disapproval.* "Back in line, 'General' Mil. That is all we need from you. After this, you will be escorted to your assigned troops."

The Purist turned to give him a firm nod, and he weakly returned it, before falling back in line. Bolios shook him by his shoulders, and Mil let out a laugh as he was released. "Good thing to know your taste hasn't worsened!"

A loud shush emerged from the speaker, and Bolios rolled his eyes, but quieted up. Mil's mind wandered to other places, though. He would be meeting his troops today. Would they respect him, with his sudden promotion?

—

"This is as far as I can take you boys. Be safe out there, alright?" Monbek scrunched his face up, and despite his efforts, Mil could make out the signs of wrinkles. Signs of age. But he couldn't see the plague on his mentor's face, not when tears welled in his eyes. *At the thought of them leaving.*

"As if we'd be anything else." Bolios smirked at Monbek, and Monbek returned the gesture.

"Be careful there Bolios, you may be tough as nails, but you still are the second." Hearty laughing broke out from Monbek, but Mil swore he could see the ghost of a frown on Bolios's face. Soon enough though, he was cheered up, and they were bantering again.

Mil didn't intrude on their bantering, and he knew it wasn't his place. He was content to stand and watch, crossing his arms as his mind fled to other matters. He looked at the wagon on the other side of the hill, another man pacing around it. It was Monbeks ride out, and he'd have to take it soon. And once he left, they'd be on their way as well.

His thoughts were interrupted as Monbek turned to him, "Now, don't ignore me over there, boy."

"Of course not! I'm sorry, si-."

Monbek slapped his hand on his shoulder, "Now, Mil, I already told you to call me Monbek. Any Purist who demands you use their title is full of themselves, quite frankly." Monbeks nose twisted, a few Purists likely already hitting his mind.

A loud holler came from down the hill, and Monbek let out a sigh. "I guess that's my cue to go. Remember what I taught you, and you'll both be right as rain." He turned away from them, and Mil watched his back as he marched towards the wagon.

Bolios waved his fist in the air, "Let's get moving! I want to meet our new squad before sundown."

Mil didn't argue, and they set off in the opposite direction, but he let himself take a few glances back at Monbek. "What do you think they'll be like, Bolios?" When he was an acolyte, his companions were a mixed bag, but he hoped this new troop may be better. After all, it was going to be his duty to lead them.

"Friendly. Or at least they better be." He did an uppercut with his fist, and Mil let out a weak laugh.

"Yeah. You're probably right." That was how Purists were, after all. He wasn't going to be dealing with acolytes anymore, and things would be different.

Silence hung among them for the rest of the trek, and after a while of walking, he could see the outline of a fire in the distance. Around it, a group of people were gathered. He couldn't make out many details, but he was sure there were more than a dozen of them.

Bolios ran out ahead, shouting out a few words he couldn't make out over the wind. The group turned to face them, and Mil had to jog to keep pace. A lilac haired woman looked over both of them, before turning to Bolios. "You're the new General?"

Bolios let out a snort, "I wish! But I'm just the lowly second." He waved back to Mil, "He's your new General. Best not get us confused!"

The woman turned to look Mil up and down, and Mil tried to remain still. He wasn't sure what he was being checked for, but he wanted to make a good impression. *What should he say to them? Hello? Or, something more formal?*

"Oh. I see." She didn't retreat back into the crowd, but kept her gaze fixed. At that point, though, another one of the men emerged. He looked young, only past twenty or so, and he had shaggy blonde hair that had been unkempt.

He looked scrawny, and he approached them with his head lowered. He held a scroll in his hand, and passed it to Mil without a second look. Mil opened it, and on it was a golden bird with a white mask. *The Purist.* Below it were the words 'Golden Squadron'. So that was their title.

Bolios came to peak at it, but after a moment, he shot up. "Come on Mil, we shouldn't just stand here! We have a squad now." Mil closed up the scroll, and followed behind him, his eyes locked on the fire in the middle of the camp.

The woman of before turned to him, "I'm Anita." She gestured to the boy that had given him a scroll, "And that's Jasper. We came here as a pair."

Like him and Bolios, then. The other men also came, and introduced themselves one by one. Mil noted their names, even if they were numerous. Petunia, Lagas, and Kalt to name a few.

Before he knew, they were all sitting around the fire, and sharing stories from their past. Bolios was halfway through telling the tale of when he and Mil had first met.

"So I hit one of them right in the head, and all that tough guy energy went out the door! Last I saw, they were running off into the woods. Too scared to face punishment, I guess."

"But, that's how I met this runt!" He gave a firm pat to Mil, and Mil smirked as he pushed him back. He may not have been as strong as Bolios, but you bet he could give a good punch if he wanted.

A pause followed, until Anita spoke up. "We should share something as well, Jasper." Jasper gave a grin.

"You bet! I have just the story-." Anita gave him a look, and he stopped speaking, casting us a smile and shake of his head.

"Jasper and I came from Anstana." It was one of the temples down near the far south of their territory. Mil hadn't heard much of it, other than the Purist noting 'strange happenings' in that area.

"Our last patrol there, we were out scouting near Martlow. Jasper and I split off from the group, and we heard screams. When we got there, weapons were embedded through all of them, and their attackers were gone. Three purists, all taken down, and their attackers nowhere to be seen."

Anitas voice twisted, and Mil felt a pang of sympathy. He couldn't imagine seeing so much death, and of your own party nonetheless. She gave a wide smile to him as he nodded to her, and her voice recovered.

"We were sent away from Anstana after that, but I still like to ponder what could be down in those woods. It couldn't be an animal, and no peasant could take down us Purists."

Jasper didn't add anything, but frowned at Anita as she kept going. She fixed her gaze on Mil, and he squirmed. "I'm sorry to hear that, Anita. They all died honorably."

"You're right. But that's why I joined this squadron. I need to make sure something like that doesn't happen again. Can you guarantee that, General?"

"Of course! I would never let my men die." After all, the Purist had trained him well, and Bolios could take anyone in a fight. Even his recruits seemed experienced. What could possibly pose a threat to them?

Anita rose, and stepped over to him, wrapping her arms around him in a sudden hug. Mil froze, and Bolios let out a laugh as he watched them. Anita withdrew, and smiled at him once more. "Thank you, Mil."

Once she returned to her seat, another man stepped up to share, but Mil was processing the hug he had received. He couldn't remember when he ever got that gesture, and from a practical stranger no less.

But, no. Anita wasn't a stranger, she was one of his squad, and he needed to remember that. He looked back to her, and she met his gaze, shooting him a slanted smile. He snapped his gaze away, back to the storyteller, and let himself settle in.

It was going to be a long night.

Chapter 11

Ariel

Ariel traced her fingers along the fabric in front of her, a map that spanned the entire table. At the heart of it was Avatross, her home. To the far left were the Purist Territories, and she shivered at the name. She had only heard remnants of what they did, and even that scared her.

But the map cut off once it hit the oceans and mountains, like they were the borders of the world. What was beyond their expanses? Kingdoms? Creatures? Something else?

She was cut off as her teacher droned on, "Avatross, our capital, was named after the first king of the realm, Aararvos." She grabbed a piece of charcoal from the desk, drawing a frame on her board. "Through connection, he would be your great-great grandfather fifteen generations ago. In fact, the name Ariel comes from his wife, Queen Ariel the first. What exactly was she known for, princess?"

Ariel let her mind flashback to all the texts she had read. Most of the husband's wives were rather unimportant, but Queen Ariel was noteworthy. She was the one that advocated for lands to be divided between nobles that report back to the king. Prior, the king had elected governors that reported to him.

She smirked at the thought of who she was named after, and spoke up, "Queen Ariel the first instituted the policy of noble houses, and all nobles today have her to thank for it." She felt a pang of worry hit her, drowning out any pride as the teacher grumbled.

"Correct, as always Princess Ariel…"

Ariel didn't let a frown touch her face, but she leaned back to try and refocus on the map. She should be happy, she got it right after all. However, her eyes came upon something she hadn't seen before, a dragon head, put just before Avatross. She looked at it transfixed, but what was it doing on the map?

"What is this doing on the map, teacher?"

The tutor leaned over, fixing her gaze before letting out a scoff. "Great. One of those maps." Her hand snapped to one edge of the map and made quick work of it, crumpling it up into a little pile of paper.

"You'll be needing none of that Princess Ariel. It is nothing of import."

Ariel didn't voice her disagreement, but she still wondered what the beast's head could have meant. "Are we going to learn about the neighboring land today?" She had asked a few weeks prior, and the tutor had said they would get to it today. She had to admit, her curiosity was piqued about what the Purists were. How could they be so malicious and evil?

"Ah. I suppose I did promise that."

The tutor sat back down at her desk, curling her fingers together as she shifted from left to right. "You must understand this is a difficult subject to broach, Princess. The state actively learns new things about these Purists everyday, and even to us, their motives are unclear."

"I was hesitant to bring this up, because this isn't like the academic questions of before. You can't simply get a question right, you need to get all the answers right here, you need to speculate. But the king did ask me to prepare you, so I will."

Ariel settled into her seat, her fingers coming together as she tried to hide her excitement. She was learning new information for once, relevant information. Information she could do something with! *But what if she used it wrong? What if she didn't grasp it?*

"You must know that Evalkyr is much older than the Purists. While we've been around for generations, they only started a few decades ago, and their leadership hasn't changed since. They're led by the Purist, and her commanders."

She raised her hand, and her tutor called, "Yes, Princess?"

"Who are her commanders? Are they warriors, advisors, or nobles?"

"According to our accounts, we only know of two commanders, and one was a recent addition. Both are warriors, and they lead generals who have squadrons under them. Now, what questions would you ask off this?"

Ariel paused, trying to consider what she was being told. In Evalkyr, warriors didn't speak to the king as his seconds, nobles did. If the Purists acted differently, that had to imply something, but what?

Suddenly, it clicked in her mind. The Purists didn't have nobles, and their structure wasn't about governance. You didn't hear about them having senators or mayors, or really rules in place to govern the towns they conquered.

"Do the Purists have any nobles, mayors? Other groups that rule the towns they have?"

The tutor nodded to her and turned to the board, scraping out a crude likeness of the Purist on it.

"The Purist and her group are not focused on being governing bodies. The towns in their land govern themselves, but they are subservient to the weaponry the Purists carry. In this regard, it is very dissimilar from Evalkyr, and in many others."

"You may also take from this that the Purists are a warrior-like faction. They are extreme in their beliefs, and have a sole monopoly on weapons in their area. No faction has been able to oppose them, except for Evalkyr."

"And what do we know about their beliefs?"

"Their system is made around the idea of achieving purity. We don't know exactly what purity is to them, but we have a good idea. The mentally weak and the physically weak for starters. To them, they're akin to monsters."

"But why? Not everyone is made to do heavy labor or read books. How does anyone deserve to die over that?"

The teacher made an 'aha' noise, and drew another sketch on the board, this time a scratch on the Purists face.

"Now you start to see the flaws in the Purists. They don't have a clear justice system or law like we do, they only have a profile they enforce on a whim. They have no government, and at that point, they are merely a fanatical group of vagabonds."

The explanation settled on Ariel's lips, and she struggled to think about it. How could a group with no control over the towns, or basic laws, even interest in justice succeed? How could they become something that was called the rival of Evalkyr?

"But enough about history, it is time we get onto language, Princess. Now, I'm sure you've studied Keshka as I told you to?"

Ariel wanted to hold in her groan. There were three tongues in the continent, the first being Anaric or Common, that most everyone knew. It may vary in spelling and words from class, but the peasants knew it, and so did she.

Then there was Rublish, the ethnic language of a group that was quite large in Evalkyr. But with most of them speaking Common, there wasn't much of a reason for her to delve into the specifics of the language.

The third, Keshka, was not a language you would hold a conversation with. The nobility used it for ceremonies, and the church did as well, so she was expected to speak it. But that didn't make it any easier for her, with all the long and complex words it held.

"Yes, tutor." She gulped, trying to remember the words that came to her mind. *Abrinth* was the word for god, and it appeared quite frequently. Or what about *Ranald* as king?

"Good, then I expect a translation of this sentence. *Ranald a beautifuaco sasta manata tamad.*"

Ariel cringed. She knew Ranald of course, and Beautifuaco meant beautiful, but nothing else in the sentence made sense to her. The king and beautiful? That made a load of sense. Sweat came down her forehead as she twitched, and the tutor let out a huff.

"The king and his beautiful wife declare peace. Princess, that was a standard line ripped right out of the texts, and you should have understood it."

Ariel wiggled in her seat, trying to come up with a response as the teacher bore down on her, but her head snapped up as she heard her reprieve. The door opened, and a messenger walked in, keeping his head low and intent.

"I'm sorry for interrupting this, Mrs. Beck, but the king has requested the presence of his daughter at court. Princess Ariel?"

Mrs. Beck gave her a firm stare, but relented and didn't make a sound as she hopped out of her seat, eager to get out of there. The messenger turned and led the way down to where her father was, not speaking a word to her. He may have been a messenger, but he could have tried to make some conversation.

They came to a set of doors that the messenger pushed open, bowing. She escorted herself in, and a long row of chairs was set along a table. At the head of the table sat her father, and nobles took up almost every other seat.

"Ariel! Come here."

She followed without hesitation, and took the seat nearest to him, which was adorned with red fabric and cushions. The nobles all gawked at her, but her father didn't react, so neither did she.

"King, sire, are you sure this is such a good idea?"

"What do you mean, Lord Tarlans?"

"Well, usually it is only customary for the queen to attend. Having a princess attend may not be the smartest course of action."

Another one spoke up, "Exactly! And now that we're on the topic, is it wise for her to be the next heir? It is tradition for a male to inherit the throne, but we only have two female heirs. Perhaps it would be in the best interest for the king to remarry."

Everyone turned to the person who said that. Ariel looked to her father, and his face was flooding with redness, cheeks puffed out as his fist clenched around the fork he was holding. At once, all of it ruptured out in a yell.

"Leave this room, Lord Bastha. Return to your town and do not come to another meeting until you have issued the crown a proper apology. Guards, escort him out!"

The lord let out a strangled gasp as the guards approached, but he got up without complaint, and promptly left the room.

"Does anybody else have any complaints about my marital status?" Her father snapped, and Ariel tried to smile. He was good at handling the nobles, and her skin prickled at the thought of him remarrying. What about mother? She could still picture that frail figure, sitting in a room, unmoving.

"Good. Then let's move on. Bring out the meals!"

Servants flooded the corridors, and Ariel got lost in the meal that was prepared for her, but even then, she could still see some of the nobles looking her down.

Her place in the court was far from established.

CHAPTER 12

ALYX

"Blimey rats." The gatekeeper had to take a loud sip of his ale to hide his eye roll as his latest 'client' passed. They were a couple of starstruck lovers hoping to settle down and make a life for themselves, something like that, at least. Well, maybe they shouldn't choose the most war-torn place on the darned map.

He was about to prepare himself for his regular lines, trying to keep the sweetest tone before his eyes fell on the next visitor. They were wearing a long, leather cloak blocking any view of their face or body. "Lord help me."

The figure was perched right in front of the gate, and he could have sworn a dagger, or something worse, was sheathed in that cloak of theirs. If not for the ragged state of it, he may have thought it was a Purist knocking at his door. Something about this one, regardless, smelled of trouble.

"Name and papers?" The figure reached into the back of their cloak and responded by setting down a large gold coin on the desk. Sweet mother of god. He didn't see those around very often. Before he could utter another word, they had already moved past the gate and into the town.

The debate inside him was a small one. Perhaps he should have told the guards of the figure getting into the town unauthorized, but his eyes were far more drawn by the coin on his desk. He looked around him, and when he was sure nobody else was present, he stuffed the coin into his pocket. Maybe this job did have some benefits.

—

She wanted to vomit. Every which way she looked, some wealthy merchant was flaunting an item of theirs. An exotic pelt they had, a golden bracelet, or even a rare artifact, you name it. If they had it, somebody in the town was bound to see it.

Meanwhile, the shop owners were nothing more than skin and bones. Their faces were roughened, and their clothing was torn. That was the face of a citizen of Arbornail, one of hardship and poverty. It wasn't just the people that reflected that, but the city.

The walls looked like they were about to fall over as she spoke, and the streets were so uneven that every cart moved at a snail's pace. However, all of that hardly seemed to be of notice to the merchants. They loudly talked of their wealth as if it was something to be proud of.

She was regretting ever coming there, and she tried to keep her eye spied for the men from the forest. But all of them looked the same, all ugly, and all shriveled up men that shouldn't have been there.

She had to keep repeating her mantra: in and out, in and out, to avoid punching one of the bastards. She would sell what she had, take the coin, deal with the men, and leave before anybody could raise a brow.

For now though, she needed something to distract her, from all the ugliness that surrounded her. She couldn't bear looking at these rich merchants any longer. Her reprieve was in a stall she spotted.

The stall she was looking at was at the end of the row, recognizable for a few reasons. The wood had already rotted, and an old woman always ran it. Usually, the elderly wouldn't show their faces in public, but she was a stark exception.

Alyx drew two hides out of her satchel as she set them down on the counter. Alyx tried to have no reaction as the woman came into view, but her eyes wavered. The woman's skin was old and bumpy; anyone else would have seen it as a sign of sickness. But Alyx couldn't help but admire it, and how she seemed to wear it without concern.

"Yes, yes, these hides will do." She ran her hands over the hides, entranced by the warm fur below. "I'll give you four silvers." Alyx let herself draw in a silent breath. That may have been an appropriate price for each but for both? She wouldn't be close to making back the gold coin she spent to even get in here.

"For each?" The incredulous look from the woman gave Alyx enough information.

"Do I look made of money, girl? You'll be lucky to find anyone else in this town that'll offer a price even close." Alyx knew that at least some of that statement was true. The pelts should have been worth at least eight silvers, but would anyone give that?

"So that's the highest you'll go?" She was shot with a glare that seemed far more fitting on a soldier than an old woman.

"I've never been wrong with things prices before, hun. Those pelts are worth four silvers, no more, no less."

Before Alyx could open her mouth to argue, both heads swung as a small shadow emerged from the back of the stall. It was a young girl, a few years old at best, and she ran to the old woman's arm. "Mama!" She cried, and the cry was all it took for Alyx to freeze up, thankful that her wide eyes were hidden beneath the hood.

"Not now, Nora." The denial only caused the girl to grab on tighter to the woman's dress, "Food! Me hungry!" A crushing pressure fell on Alyx's chest as she watched the scene unfold, and her heart began to race as her eyes fell further upon the girl. Her ribs were showing, and she looked skinny, far too thin for a girl her age.

"I'll take the four silvers." She blurted out, and the old woman's head snapped up, as she pushed Nora towards the back. When she dropped the four silver coins onto the counter, Alyx snatched them up and turned on her heel, storming into the crowd without a second thought.

Calm down. She repeated it over and over again in her mind, but nothing seemed to happen. Instead, her mind worked against her as it ripped and tore into her memories, letting her see into the past. *There was a line of children there. They were almost as skinny as her.*

Some of them had wild and matted hair, while others had long gashes or scars. It was what happened on the farms, but to them, it was a sign of something more. *There was blood and bodies. The smell was putrid.*

Even under the house, her small eyes could see what was happening, and they were transfixed, unable to look away from the devastation happening in front of her. *Mother. Where's my mother?* She wasn't anywhere to be seen, not in the line of people or the crowd. She had simply vanished with the wind.

At that point, she covered her eyes with her hands, letting the yells echo in her ears until they finally stopped. She let her hands fall, and in front of her, two large figures stood outside the house. They started to lean down, to look at her, and then-.

Oof. She fell face-first into something, bouncing back as she ripped at her hood, trying to keep her face sealed even as she soared. "Ay! Watch where you're going!" Her eyes fell upon who she had run into. *No. Not them!*

Two Purists stood before her, their white robes adorned with golden markings as they scrutinized her with what she swore was ire. Looking at their robes, she wanted to rip hers and burn it into a thousand pieces, but she couldn't. That would surely seal her fate.

"Sorry." She tried to make it past them, but one of them reached out to grab her arm, yanking her back to where she was.

"Now, who exactly are you, missy?" *Remember, they're nothing. You've met worse men.* The justification was bitter on her tongue, but she stood up straight, puffing out her chest to meet them.

"Alyx." The two exchanged a look, a giggle coming from one of them. "Alyx, who? You certainly don't look like a noble to me."

She shook her head, "I'm a local hunter. Is there anything I can do for you two, or will you continue to hold me up?"

The silence was agonizing, but she refused to let herself cower. *They prey on the weak. Show yourself to be strong, and they'll be too scared to even face you.* "You wouldn't mind taking that cloak off, now?" The suspicion that rolled from their gazes set her back a step.

How could they have known? She was hardly at Arbornail, and when she did come, it was spaced out. "And why should I do that? Last I checked, you aren't the guards."

A snort emerged from one of them as they looked around before hollering to a nearby guard. "You! Lad! Over here!"

The man trotted over right away, and then she realized she wouldn't get out of this one. Not easily, at least. "Happy? Now take off that cloak, and we can all be on our merry way." No. She wasn't going to let this happen to her. Not again.

She looked to the alleyway to her side, and before any of them could react, she kicked at the sand below, darting off to the right.

"Stop her!" A voice yelled from behind, and she didn't care to look back and see who it was. Her hands hurriedly went to shed the cloak, throwing it behind her so she could run at a sprint.

"Go left." Her eyes bulged when she heard the voice, sure it wasn't from anyone nearby. Her head swung, trying to figure out where it came from, but all she was met with was an angry stampede of guards heading in her direction.

Her mind raced between two separate paths, one being what the voice was and the second, the guards who were about to catch her if she didn't act fast. So she cast aside her judgment and spun her head to look to her left.

There. A small opening was present, and without a second thought, she dove into it. She stopped breathing, waiting as she saw one guard pass by her, the next, and the next. But only when the footsteps were mere echoes in the town did she emerge, breathing as she panted.

"Up. The exit is up." Her head moved up; low and behold, a ladder led up to the rooftops, and those led right to the front of the city. She decided she would ponder more about why she was hearing things later when she wasn't worried about Purists and guards trying to capture her and, for all she knew, skin her.

She hoisted herself up the ladder, and as her feet pressed against the tiles of the ceilings, she let a smile bless her face. It seemed her luck hadn't run out yet; hopefully, it wouldn't anytime soon.

—

BENJAMIN

"Commander, sir." Benjamin was grooming his beard when two underlings barged in without a knock. He was about to turn around and scream at them, but he paused when he noticed their faces. Something was amiss.

"What is it?" He snapped, and the two bowed their heads, stuttering their words as they tried to speak. "We- we found plague in the city of Arbornail. We were trying to capture it, but it somehow eluded the guards, and well..."

"Plague? In the heart of Arbornail?" What an absurd suggestion. He had carved out any remnant of that more than a decade ago, and he would not have his hard work doubted. "You must be mistaken, disciples, or have you forgotten our cleansings already?"

With a triumphant smile, Benjamin returned to getting rid of all the knots in his beard, but his barons seemed willful. A bit too intentional at that. "It's true, sir! I swear by my life, the plague- its skin was too pale to be human, its hair was white, but it was hardly an elder! And the eyes, they were like a snake, blood red!"

He stopped abruptly, his eyes falling open as his hands fell loose, his comb falling to the floor. He turned to face the two disciples; for now, his eyes looked like the red ones. "What did you just say?"

CHAPTER 13

MIL

Mil let out a groan as he got up from a not so restful night of slumber. The last few months had been a blur. After getting to know each other, they had trekked from the temple all the way out to the border, and set up camp. A few weeks had gone by, and things were normal. But then they got into the ale, and everything went downhill from there.

Mud and dust were splattered everywhere. It was probably the most exciting thing to be seen in the barren land they were stationed in, with not a single hill nor blade of grass in sight.

Mil couldn't bring himself to be mad, because he wasn't doing any better. Things weren't the same now that he wasn't at the temple. He should have been reasonable and not gotten into the ale, but a bit of indulgence couldn't have hurt, right? It's not like the Purist Codes had a rule against it.

His gaze lightened though when he saw Bolios, picking up a barrel and putting it back into place as he laughed with another one of the men. When he saw Mil, he waved over, letting out a yell.

"I tried to stop them, sir! I truly did! But you know them, they wake up on the wrong side of the bed, and it'll all be over!" Laughter broke out at his 'plead,' and Mil couldn't help but be amongst them.

"Don't rat us out yet!" One of the soldiers yelled, poking his stick at Bolios, who fell over as if he had been stabbed. "He got me! General, please, I beg for your help!" Mil didn't realize the group had gotten so close to Bolios, and he stroked his beard in thought. He should go along with their little game.

"It seems my hand is forced, Bolios. You were a good second in command!" Mil turned back to his tent, secretly a bit happy he may be able to wake up more before the day's antics began. He couldn't help but smirk at the cries of Bolios. He really was playing along with them.

As Mil fled to the back of his tent, he started to rummage through his supplies, reminiscing on everything he had there. He had lost a lot of his feeling of home when he left, after all, he'd lived his whole life at the temple, but his objects never changed. They were his sole comfort.

He let his hand droop down his bag, and once he felt a cold chill against his hand, he immediately knew what he had found. A grin crossed his face as he yanked it up, being greeted with a stone compass. Not just any compass, however, but the one had been gifted when he was promoted to General by the Purist herself.

A griffin and manticore were carved out on its sides, battling one another. It was almost like a replica of the Purist's halls; the material alone spoke its value. He was shocked the Purist would be willing to part from it, but he decided not to question a good deed. After all, he was making sure to take good care of it. It was too exquisite for anything less.

Plus, it brought back good memories. Now that he was out here, he hardly got to see the Purist anymore, but he still read her letters, and he wished they could go back to having the discussions they used to. She always seemed prepared, and no matter what point he'd make, she'd retort with an argument that'd make him reconsider everything he'd said prior.

But she was right about another thing: everything had checks and balances. He may not have the serious discussions that he used to anymore, but instead, he got to lay back and enjoy his time at the border. He didn't like the gruel of the work, but unlike the other Purists, they weren't bothered by plague or attacks.

He sighed as he put the compass into his bag, hoisting it over his shoulder as he prepared to exit for the day. But he froze when he emerged from his tent as his men were standing in line, facing two dismounting riders. He wasn't expecting anybody, but they were decked in Purist attire.

The two riders were lined with steel armor, although it was more for show than anything anyone would use in combat. Precise openings were present in their faces and chest, likely to let their achievements show, while gold lining and patterns were on the outside.

"General Mil at your service." He moved to the front, saluting the two men with a sloppy wave. The first looked him over with a scrutinizing glare, while the other snorted as he leaned further into his mount. "We bring news from Commander Benjamin that he considers of utmost importance."

A whirl of confusion struck Mil, as to start, he wasn't expecting any news, and certainly not so soon after they got there. Not to mention that his battalion was under Commander Trisha, not Benjamin. Indeed there must have been a mix-up, but he let his eyes fall upon the yellow badges on the two's chests.

"Of course, sirs. Shall we move to my tent?" They spoke no further, which indicated to Mil that they had no objections. He waved to Bolios, who moved to his side, his nose and mouth cracked sideways. It would have been invisible to the naked eye, but to Mil, he knew his second was currently holding back his tongue.

Now that he wasn't being brought out of his tent as soon as morning cracked, he could admire how nice it was compared to his men. His sleeping bag was splayed out with various furs, and the extra room tent had been filled with makeshift seats that, in truth, were little more than logs. They had gone neglected, but it seemed they finally had a purpose.

He and Bolios took the front two, but the men made no motion to sit, instead staying up and standing. The two exchanged a look, and Mil was unsure why the two seemed to be acting standoffish at best. "Is something the matter?"

The first one slammed a scroll down onto one of the logs, nodding to it. "A plague born has been spotted in the city of Arbornail. The local guards could not track it, so your squadron will be sent out. Bring its head to Commander Benjamin."

"Is Commander Trisha aware of this?" Mil tried to hide his disappointment at the news; after all, they had been assigned to a relaxing post, and now they were being sent off on a plague hunt. They'd have to trek down there, hunt the plague, then trek all the way up to the temple again.

"We would not be here otherwise. You will now be reporting to Commander Benjamin as your commanding officer." Mil had never heard of a squadron being switched to another officer; usually, once one was assigned, it stayed until the Commander left their post. He couldn't help the concern that came to him, was this meant to be a punishment? Had his squadron not been performing up to Purist standards?

"And what rank are you two pretty boys? Certainly not high enough to speak on behalf of Commanders, I sure as hell bet!" Mil wheezed as soon as Bolios finished, his friends antics at it again.

"Now, now, I'm sure what Bolios was meaning to say is that this is quite the shock to us all; Commander Trisha never signaled to us there would be a switch."

Bolios snapped his gaze over to him, and the two men seemed impassive until the first one smirked. "If you must know, we are

Commander Benjamin's chosen disciples. You, meanwhile, are the second-in-command to one of the border Generals, no?" The scathing tone caused even Mil to flinch, especially as the man's tongue reached his title as a 'border General.'

And as for the rest of his speech? He may have just run out of the tent at that second. These weren't acolytes or even messengers but disciples. And ones hand-picked by one of the Commanders, no less. While Mil was defending their borders and relaxing in his tent, these disciples were being groomed for Commandership and likely having elaborate dinners with the Purist herself!

And he thought that having a few discussions with the Purist every year or so amounted to anything. These people were at the top of the ladder, and his second had insulted their authority. He swore he could feel a dagger in his heart as he started to melt under the gazes of the two men as if they expected him to do something in response.

It was too much, and he remained silent, trying to keep his gaze at Bolios. His friend was his one rock in that time, as he kept his gaze firm on the two disciples, but they both frowned at him. "General Mil, I must say, we are quite disappointed in the treatment we have received, and from your second no less. Do you intend to do something about this?"

His eyes wafted over to the disciples, who both smiled as they looked at Bolios, seemingly satisfied. He felt the panic in his chest nearly explode and he couldn't move his lips. He needed to do his job as General, but what was he meant to do? Bolios was his friend, but the Purist Code called him to do something.

"I will talk to Bolios after this. I promise you that disciples."

The first one smirked, "Ah, ah, your second, best you remember that we call ourselves by formal titles, General."

The second one let the words sink in, before speaking, "I should suppose our business here is done then, General.

Although, I must say though, I would advise you reconsider your taste in seconds." Bolios and the man had a silent feud between them as they glared back, each having a hurl of words on their tongue but sheathing them to not be heard. "Yes. I suppose it is. Thank you, disciples."

The two left without another word, and once they were left alone, Bolios turned to him, his goofy attitude gone for a serious one. "What was that about Mil? They came into our camp, treated us like scum, and you tell them you're going to 'handle' me? I was sticking up for you!"

"That's not it! Don't you get it, Bolios? There are rules here! And those disciples outrank us by a mile! What they say goes, and it isn't our place to question them whenever we like." He froze, "You're my second Bolios! What you do reflects on me, and now all the disciples will hear about this."

"So this is about you now, Mil? Look beyond yourself! All you had to do was ask for a confirmation letter, and those idiots would provide it if they weren't full of shit! Do you really take whatever someone says as fact?"

Mil shot up, his fists crunching together as a million thoughts ran through his head. Why didn't Bolios understand? There were rules here! And he seemed to think it was his fault for not breaking them? "Stop it!"

Bolios came to a standstill as he looked up at him, his fists untightening as if he was a child being scolded by a parent. "I can't believe you, Bolios. I knew you didn't always like authority, but this was going too far."

Bolios's jaw unhinged, and he growled, "You'll see that I'm right Mil. They'll come back and push you around now forever if you keep letting them. Does it even matter if they were telling the truth? They were treating you like a pest, all while you hunt their plague for them!"

Before he could retort any further, his former second marched out of the tent, and he heard a ruckus in the camp as a few shouts rang out, followed by Bolios's voice.

He turned away from the front of the tent, his eyes landing on the scroll the disciples had left. A map, maybe? Or a plan of how they'd get to Arbornail? His hands glided across the surface, and only then did he realize how exquisite the paper was, something no standard message would be carried on.

He unraveled it, and in it, a long message was encoded in the blackest of ink, and as soon as he read the first line, his entire body froze up. *The plague born was to be captured. Alive.* The disciples had told him that he was to kill the plague born. But why not say to him that while they were here instead of passing it off to a scroll?

He looked at the empty log beside him, and suddenly it clicked. Bolios was with him then, and they had put the scroll to him, not his former second. They didn't want his men or even his second to know whatever was contained on this scroll.

CHAPTER 14

ARIEL

"Oh, stand still won't you?" Her maid fussed as she tied the ribbon at her back together, while another gave splashes of color to her cheeks. Ariel could only smile as she looked back at her reflection, her hair braided into an elaborate pattern while her makeup shined on her face. Not to mention her dress, which seemed to speak radiance with its mere presence.

"Simply gorgeous." This time it was her handmaiden, Bessa, wisping her fingers through her hair as she steadied her. "Not a single suitor wouldn't look at you now." Oh. Right. Ariel tried to hide the frown that came to her face at the word, instead projecting a bright smile.

"Who do you think they'll be? I heard there's so many coming!" *Nobody should be coming. Nobody.* "Well, I did hear that the Arbornails have a specially handsome boy." The other maid shook her head, huffing, "What good is a family that doesn't have their own territory? Not anymore, at least."

Bessa shushed the other maid, and though she feigned ignorance, Ariel knew what they were talking to. Her father had told her that they were fighting the Purists back at the border with ease, but she heard what the maids and servants whispered. The purists had already taken Arbornail and Fieldmoor, what would be next?

94

But she knew she couldn't ask that. She had far more important things to do than to worry or doubt her father. So instead, she acted like it was a joke, laughing as if the servants had told her of a farce. She didn't need to be told it was all too real.

"All done, my lady. Shall we escort you to the ballroom?" *No. Couldn't you just leave me alone?* "Of course, Bessa. You've been so kind today." She let her head hang low as the maids flanked her on either side, leading her down the long hallway. It never seemed to change, like it itself was a maze.

But when instead of the carpet, she saw an unkempt, although not ragged, girl in a worn dress and she froze. The girl was no impoverished beggar, but she hardly reflected that of a royal.

And Ariel knew exactly who she was. Nemona. Bessa stepped in front of her, her nose snarling up at the sight of Nemona, as if an unpleasant thing had stepped in her path. Nemona seemed to have no reaction, her frowning before staying strong.

"This way, your highness." They crowded around her like a pack of dogs, not so much as acknowledging Nemona as they walked away from her.

"Stop."

She yelled out, and all the maids froze in their spots. She turned to look at Nemona, who paused, looking at her with wide eyes. "Nemona? Where have you been? I haven't seen you forever!"

Ariel threw her arms around Nemona, smiling. It took a moment, but Nemona returned the gesture, and they were hugging again. Ariel wanted to ask more, but she didn't want to interrupt the moment either. Her maids, apparently, didn't get that message.

"Ahem, Princess Ariel, the ball is waiting. Your father will be upset if you're late."

Ariel didn't want to stop the hug, but she also didn't want to make her father mad. "Come to my room later, Nemona. Alright?"

Nemona looked to the maids before her, but nodded. "Of course. Enjoy your ball, Ariel." Nemona hesitated as she moved back, but turned and continued her walk nonetheless. Ariel frowned, turning to glare at her maids.

What's up with them today? Why were they snubbing her? When they reached the ballroom, the maids opened the door, and she moved her head up, one hand holding her dress while the other fell to her side.

A grand orchestra of music came to her as musicians from all around played their instruments, and Ariel had to use all her willpower to not cover her ears and balk. *The noise. It's too much. Too much.* She walked down the carpet, looking down at all the noble guests that were fraternizing and sharing drinks.

They all watched her, some with hunger, and others with curiosity, like scavenging vultures sizing up her value. To the other side, sat the thrones, of which there were three of them. The biggest one sat her father, who was hardly recognizable behind all his garments.

He wore a long robe that touched to the floor, and on his head, sat an ornate crown littered with jewels, while his face was shadowed by his long, shaggy hair. To his left, was a slightly smaller throne, and Ariel's heart fell when she looked at it.

It was meant to sit the queen, in all her glory, next to her king, but mother wasn't in it. Instead, it was dusty and old, scratches meeting its basin. The third one was that of silver, and it was both as terrifying as her fathers, and as small as her mothers. It was her throne, and without any control, she felt her legs carrying her to it.

She sat down on the hard metal, not showing her discomfort as her dress bundled up behind her, and her arms clung to the sides of it for dear life as she looked at the room ahead of her. It was massive, and the crowd was so large that it was impossible to make out anyone's individual features without straining her eyes.

They all blurred into one mass upon the white marble floors, only hurting her eyes more as the bright colors flashed against them. Now she truly remembered why she hated the ballroom so much, and these events as a whole.

The ceilings also towered above her, and she averted her eyes, feeling a pang of anxiety as her mind scrambled to process the large hall in front of her. *Focus. Focus. It's not too much, you can do it.* She tried to lie to herself like that all the time. And then she lied again when she told herself that it worked.

"Nobles of Evalkyr! We are blessed to have you all in our presence, and in such a mass! Why, it makes my eyes joyful to see so many of you before us once again!" Her father held up his glass of wine, and the nobles before them did the same, cheering erupting as they all took a large slurp of it.

"Now, am I so pleased to announce that we may start with the gifts!" Of course. It was an old tradition that nobles from across the land would present their finest trinkets to them, but that didn't make it any more interesting. She watched as her father called out various names, and they wheeled up everything you could imagine.

Berries, gold, books, wines, if one was adventurous perhaps even live creatures. Depending on her father's reaction, the maids would either leave the gifts or take them to a resting place. Not many caught her eye, in truth, beyond a hound, but it left just as quickly as it came.

"And at last, the Arbornail family!" A heavy silence carried, before the crowd started to part in waves, and a wheeling sound could be heard as a large statue came into view, pushed by servants on a cart. Ariel's jaw dropped at its pure size, and as it approached her, the details were clearer.

It was like a lizard, of some kind, but giant, and it stood on two like a human. Its wings fanned out as it roared to them, as if it was truly a massive, and real beast that was in front of them. She could only vaguely recall something like it from a fairytale she read as a child. It was so life-like.

She looked to her father, who stroked his beard, as if unsure on how to react to the gift. "And what is this, exactly?" One of the nobles stepped forward, and he seemed to be a middle aged man- the head of his family, if Ariel had to guess.

"Why, my king, we wish to present you with an ancient relic of our family- a statue of one of the creatures that used to walk these lands, thousands upon thousands of years ago. It was created only by the most skilled of hands."

Ariel was sucked into the statue, and to her, it seemed like a perfect gift to adorn the front of the palace, or something similar. But her father seemed less impressed. "And what do you suggest we do with this statue, Bire? It barely fits into our ballroom, let alone our castle."

Whispers broke out among the nobles as this 'Bires' face fell, and his face seemed to take on a more stone-cold look. "We would not offer such a gift if it was anything short of perfection. I am sure it would do well in your castle, to show off the might of Evalkyr."

Her father seemed as if he was about to reject the gift, but before anything further could happen, she blurted the first words that came to her mind out. "I'll take it." Everyone in the room seemed to change their direction to face her, and Bire smiled, almost a bit too much.

"Why, of course, my princess. We would be happy to bestow the statue upon you." He bowed down in a sign of respect, as his servants pushed the statue forward, and suddenly, she froze up, unsure of what to do as it approached her. She felt a draw to the statue, and the intricate design, but what was she to actually do with it?

Her father seemed to take it in stride, he wasn't about to deny the gift. "Yes, yes, I am sure it'll serve my daughter well. Thank you, Bire." Bire slinked to the back of the crowd with that, and the gifts continued, with her mind racing. *You shouldn't have said that.* But it worked out, didn't it? *Did you see all their eyes on you? Watching? Ready to tear you apart?*

She fell further back into her chair, trying to remain regal as she cowered from the attention the room projected forward. Her father continued to mutter out things, thank yous for gifts, and whatnot, but it barely registered in her mind. She instead looked to the statue she had 'earned', and specifically at the face of the beast, with its many teeth and claws.

"I can see you too, little one."

She nearly jumped back in fright, staring at the statue again and again, but there was nothing more, only the continuing drawls of the royals and her father. Maybe she really was starting to go insane. *You can't. Did you forget already? You're a princess. The princess.*

And as she only proceeded to nod at every further gift, smiling as if it was the best day in her life, she pushed the thought of that voice out of her mind. She grabbed her own glass of wine as soon as it was offered, and took down large gulps as she raised it up. But as she looked up, drowning out what she felt, she could see a single figure standing on the platforms, Nemona.

And she was looking right at her.

CHAPTER 15

"I must humbly disagree with your findings. I have observed the plague for many years, and though beastly on the outside as they are, the inside yields different results. Yes, I do claim I have seen them cry over their deceased loved ones, just as I have seen them work for their fair keep. So I must ask, why do you ignore this fact?"

- Disgraced Purist Scholar, whose name was lost to time

ALYX

Once she was out of the city, all she could do was pace one foot after another, trying to forget anything else around her. Still, she couldn't forget the screams and panic she heard as she left. She knew the Purists, and she knew that they wouldn't let this go.

She just had to hope that anger was directed to her, and not everyone inside of Arbornail. She felt a sinking sense inside of her as the whole situation dawned on her. She had managed to escape for over a decade from the Purists, and now they were after her. Again.

It was only after she could no longer see the town, now all engulfed by the forest, that she stopped at last. She didn't know what she felt at that point, but only that it was all bubbling up into her, so she reacted in the best way she could.

With clenched fists, she spun around and hit the nearest target, a tree. As soon as her hand collided with the bark, a sting of pain shot through her and she recoiled, looking over her now purple and red hand.

Her emotions always seemed to be a curse to her. First, she gave away her only hide for four silvers, then she got caught by the Purists because of it. Now, she hurt her hand, and all for what? Surely, nobody else had to suffer like this. No, instead they waltzed through life, as if they could turn their emotions off at will.

She turned back to the same tree, and let loose. She only could feel the burning of her hands as they collided with the trees, but it served to distract from everything else. *They found her. Now how was she meant to run? They'd never let her go free.*

It was all becoming a blur as she focused on her now bloodied hands, until something fell upon her, a sense she wasn't alone. She swung around, her arms ready to continue their tirade, until she saw who it was.

An old woman was standing there, clothed in a fine hide, and recognition hit Alyx, so that her blur vanished. Now, she could feel the ache and grime on her hands, who looked as if they had been smashed in by a club.

But what interested her, and terrified her, more, was who the woman was. She was the same as the one from the stand, and she scrutinized Alyx as if she had encountered a wild unicorn, before a large smile broke out on her face.

"And I suppose you have a rather logical reason for punching a tree in the middle of the woods?" How was she meant to reply to that? Of course she didn't, but would she really tell the woman that? And why was she even here, so far from the town? Had the Purists sent her?

"Who are you? Why are you here?" The old woman tilted her head, popping her lips together as she took a few steps back, her eyes wandering over Alyx. Even though she could tell the old woman was no threat on her own, it seemed like she could hardly stand without hunching forward.

"Well, I do have a name, but I doubt that matters to you. And as for why I'm here, the same reason as you, I presume. Foraging." Alyx wished that was the reason she was here, but she nodded, deciding she wasn't going to say anything yet. If the old woman thought she had nothing to do with the Purists, she wanted to keep it that way.

"So far from the city? And alone?" Alyx couldn't huddle down her suspicion at the old woman. After all, any person who actually had a brain wouldn't be out and about like this. Certainly not at her age, either. Not to mention how fast they managed to reach there.

"Where else would you recommend I go? Last I checked, the city sure ain't growing berries out of its walls. And no, I'm not." As if on cue, a small figure burst from the bushes, looking between them as the old woman waved her over.

It was the girl from the shop, and now that Alyx could get a better look at her, she saw something unexpected in her eyes, strength. Although she was far too skinny, the girl still seemed to have the energy of any child, and the curiosity of one as well.

"Now, I may not be a doctor, but I can sure as hell say those hands ain't looking so good. And I imagine you don't have the coin to pay one of the village healers."

Alyx did not. Her four silvers may have gotten her a check up at best, but certainly not bandages with the supply they likely had. And, that was assuming she'd even go back to the village to begin with.

"What does it matter to you? I'll get healing at the next town over." She could. Probably. If she made another good kill, and went to one of the less affected towns. But she'd have to avoid the

Purists as well. That may mean she had only one option, and she shivered at the idea.

"Not on my watch, missy. I'm not about to let you make those wounds even worse." She nodded to the little girl, who began to move towards the grassy side of their patch, and the old woman followed her. "Hurry up! I may change my mind if you keep us waiting."

The two continued to walk on, before disappearing behind the foliage, and Alyx was left there shocked, trying to process what she was being told. Her hands were sore, and she didn't know if she could be going to the towns anytime soon.

Oftentimes, she didn't have to deal with injuries, as she had learned how to avoid them early on. At least, nothing beyond what a simple bandage couldn't fix. But did she know that'd work this time?

Finally, it was the new surge of pain that hit her hands which caused her to lumber forward. She tried to follow the path the two seemed to go on, but found that despite the two's varying ages, they had made it far faster than her.

There was no clear path beneath her, only a narrow opening where the trees and bushes didn't touch. It was nothing like what you may expect to lead to a town, and she likely would have mistaken it for another part of the forest.

She didn't know how long it took to get through there, but it felt like an eternity, until at last, the bushes began to fade, and light shined through the cracks. The forest began to clear itself, instead making a hilly meadow, where at the top, a log cabin sat.

It was nothing extravagant, but it was hardly a run down tent, either. She tentatively approached it, peeking through the windows as she saw the old woman scrubbing away at some dishes, and the little girl sitting down.

Nothing was off about it, and so, she took in a deep breath and knocked upon the door. She had to stop herself from cringing back as soon as her hands contacted the wood.

The door flew open, and the woman let out a huff, "Took you long enough! Now get inside, I already have everything ready." Alyx couldn't reply before she was yanked inside, and promptly sat down on the nearest chair, looking right into the eyes of the little girl.

A plate was in front of her, with a serving of meat on it, while the old woman opened a box. Various vials and cloths were mixed around inside it, and she wielded them with precision.

Alyx gritted her teeth as the woman started by rubbing a balm on her hands, then ripped out a few cloths, tying them together neatly. It almost made her look like she had gloves, rather than bandages, if not for the blood that was slowly staining into its fabric.

"Now eat! I don't need anymore antics from you." With that, the woman took a seat and both her and the girl started to dig in, while Alyx was left staring in shock. She was at a dinner table with two others, like a family.

"I didn't make you a serving just for you to stare at it, ya know." Oh. Right. Alyx reached out and began to rip chunks off, stuffing it in her mouth as the two's jaws dropped to her.

"Goodness gracious, girl, use your silverware!" Alyx's eyes fell to the two silver utensils on the table, things that she had hardly seen for the majority of her life. She was meant to use them? Why?

The woman let out a dramatic sigh, "Nora, take your plate to your room. I need to talk to our guest." The girl grabbed the plate and left without a complaint, leaving Alyx even more bewildered at the situation that was unfolding in front of her, and how fast it was moving.

"You're a mystery, aren't you hun? First you leave in such a hurry, then you're punching a tree, and now you can't use silverware? I'm not blind, girl."

"And now the Purists are all up in arms, saying a 'plague' has breached Arbornail. You may want to start explaining, dear."

Of course. It was back to this. "And what if I am? You think the Purists would do you any favors? They'd probably call you a plague themselves!"

"I never said they wouldn't. You'd be deaf if you think anyone in Arbornail actually likes em folk. But I've never seen the Purists get all riled up like this."

Alyx didn't know how to reply. Why would she be any different from the rest of the innocents the Purist slaughtered? Were they really so sure they'd rooted out their imaginary plague?

"Why do you go to Arbornail then? You know it's crawling with Purists!"

The old woman sat down her cup, leaning up into her chair. "Hun, if I left every time some self-important fool came to me, I'd have nowhere left to go."

No. Nobody could be as foul as the Purists. They were an anomaly, not a rule. "I'd advise you to do the same. You look nothing more than flesh and bones. You can even stay here if you'd like."

She could stay? In their cabin? But why? She didn't know what to think of the offer, or even what it may expect of her, but in that moment, she felt something actually good. Like a bubbling in her chest. *Maybe emotions are not all bad.*

CHAPTER 16

MIL

Thunder boomed above them as the rain poured into the valley below. Everything was soaked, and Mil would cringe as his cloak sagged onto him, now little more than a damp rag. Even the horses had started to complain, stamping their feet and rearing in protest.

He couldn't say his men were much happier. This time, nobody rode at his side, and he swore his back was being met with glares. He knew why. They all had expected to stay at their post, not be sent on a plague hunt.

He'd never say it out loud, but even he felt wary from the storms and terrain they were to bear. Or that this would be his first ever plague hunt. He had the luxury of guarding the borders or maintaining order in the towns, rather than having to do the dirty work that came with being a Purist. Until now that is.

Another boom sounded above, and he took that as a signal they couldn't weather the night for much longer. "Tack off everyone! We'll stop here for the night." With that he slid off his horse, and tied it to the nearest tree.

The rest was a flurry of chaos, as dozens of feet thundered to get the camp set up in the bleak weather. Soon enough Mil found himself behind a growing fire, roasting away his worries as he stared at the cooking meal.

Two men were at either side of him, but his fire was rather empty, and he struggled to decide if that was good or bad. For now, he tried to focus on the rather absurd ghost story Jasper was weaving, his voice arching loud enough so the whole forest could hear.

"You see, they always did say this stretch of the map was haunted! But nobody ever tells you why that is. It must have been nearly a thousand years ago, when the empire was still around. They were at their prime, and Evalkyr was nearly brought to their knees! A shame, because it wasn't to last."

Mil's head whipped around as Jasper continued to speak, his jaw hitting the ground in surprise. He knew what he was talking about. When he and the Purist used to debate, she referenced the old empire. She told him how it was a glorious place, but nothing can last forever.

It was beyond him, however, how Jasper, who wasn't high up from what he could tell, knew about it. Now he was intent to listen to this tale, one that was fresh even to his ears, and others were as well. He took a sip of his stew, nearly sputtering it out from the bitterness alone, but soon he was entranced back into the elaborate story.

Anita cut in as the story continued, "Don't bore them with your old ghost stories, Jasper. There's a reason I'm always the one telling stories." Jasper quirked an eyebrow at her, but unlike before, he didn't relent.

"A beast walked these forests, a concoction of nature itself. Some said it was a lion, others a snake, and the most creative, a dragon. But what was known was that whenever somebody creeped to this valley, it would fall deathly silent. The next thing they knew, it would appear, and those sorry folk would never be heard of again."

Murmurs broke out amongst them, and Bolios tilted his head in the crowd, "And what happened to the beast? I would rather not have to deal with that on this sorry vacation." A few men nodded, and some even looked frightened at the prospect.

Jasper turned to him, letting a grin rest on his lips as he nodded. "Who knows? The beast seems as elusive as the men that visited it. Whatever happened, you can see this valley is nothing but a husk now." Mil let his gaze levy to Bolios, but once he saw Mil, he shook his head and moved back into the crowd. So they still weren't on speaking terms.

Jasper turned to look at everyone then, as if waiting for a cue from them, when Mil felt a sharp pang against his head. A cube of ice rattled off, and more followed as he scurried under the tree. He let disbelief take him, hail? In these parts?

"Perhaps we best head in. We wouldn't like to get frostbite." It was Jasper again, and Mil couldn't bring himself to disagree as more cold pangs hit him. He lurched up, finding his body rather sluggish as he dragged himself to the nearest tent.

He found himself not caring about finding the right one, instead collapsing on the bed as soon as he could, relief settling over him, but before he could drift into the realms of sleep, he paused. Someone had left a warm bowl of soup by his bed.

He wasn't that hungry, but he wasn't the kind of man to rebuke a gift. He grabbed the bowl and took a few sips, his throat burning at the bitter flavor. He put it down soon after, already not a fan of the taste.

Oh well. I'll just tell them I fell asleep before I could eat it. With that, he turned in for the night.

———

When Mil next awoke, he was in the valley again. The sun was high, and he was alone. He swiveled as best he could, but all he could see was grass stretching in every which way, and in the distance, the peaks of mountains.

"Jasper!" No one came to answer him, so he yelled and yelled again, until finally he was even calling upon Bolios, displeasure building in his chest at that fact. But it felt that every time he called someone, his throat got tighter and tighter, until he could only let out a gasp.

It was then, when he fell silent, that he could feel the shaking beneath him, and the hot breath landing on his shoulder. He turned, his feet carrying him back as fast as he could, and his eyes locking onto the great mass above him.

It would have looked like a giant lion to the untrained eye, but he knew what it was. A scorpion's tail on the back, and two wings at its sides. He was face to face with a manticore. He tried to reach out his hand, to feel the beast's mane, but it was at that moment, its cheeks curled back.

He leapt back, and it was at that moment that it lurched forward. Its paws slammed into the ground in front of him, and the earth gave way, cracking beneath it. He bolted, urging his legs to run as fast as they could as thuds followed behind him.

He didn't need to imagine what would happen if it caught him, for now he could truly see. What he thought was a noble creature was simply no more than a savage predator looking for something to fill its belly.

He was only able to run for what he thought was a minute, before he felt a sharp pain in his side and he fell. A heavy weight made its way on his chest, and his hands reached up to the manticore's massive paw, trying his hardest to lift it off.

Its blue eyes bore into his own, and it watched him, as if it found this little game amusing. He braced himself for the impact, when it decided it had enough, but it never came. Instead, the creature morphed. What he once thought looked like a lion's head, now mimicked a mans.

Its mouth opened and closed, as if it was speaking, but everytime it made a sound, the wind took it, leaving only a ringing in his ear. At last, it lowered itself so that its massive head was near his, and whispered into his ear, before jamming its paw right into his chest.

"Why won't you hear me?"

—

His eyes burst open as he coughed and sputtered, liquid pooling out of his mouth as he tried to ready himself. His vision was blurry, but he could see a group of figures crouched around him, and vaguely make out their speech.

"Get more doses! He isn't going to make it at this rate!" They shot phrases back and forth as he continued to sputter, feeling a vile sense of dread as at last, the liquid clogging his throat was coughed up. At that, his head began to clear, and he could see who was around him.

Jasper was at one side, while Anita was at another, and he swore he could see another shadow at the front of the tent.

"Oh dear lord! General!"

Anita dove down to hug his side, causing him to sputter more as she withdrew. "What happened?" He got out, his voice weak as he looked between the two, who's voices both went pale. They were both faint, and Mil felt the same. He didn't know what was more terrifying to him. His dream, or the reality he was waking up to.

"We're not sure, sir. Suddenly you just started convulsing, and you looked as if you were on death doors. But then you woke up."

His dread spiked as he heard her speak. What could that possibly mean? Was he being inflicted by an illness now, of all times? And what about his dream?

He turned his gaze to Jasper, who now seemed to look a lot more boyish than before. His face was clean-shaven, his blonde hair spilling out in uncared locks, and his innocence radiating like beams off of him.

"Jasper, do you remember the story you told me?" Jasper tilted his head, his eyebrows furrowing. Mil felt despair creep through him. Was he going crazy? He was sure Jasper was the one that told that story. Nearly everyone was listening too.

"What story, General?" He let out a rasp of disbelief, letting his mind fall back to the night, and he tried to push himself up. He mumbled out the first words he could muster.

"You know the one! The cursed valley, and the beast. You told it!" Jasper reeled back, his eyes pulling away like he had been slapped.

"I don't know what you're talking about, sir." The meagerness in his voice caused Mil to pause, and he laid back down.

Anita shot a glare to Jasper, and he shut his mouth right away. She turned back to Mil, a softer expression coming to her face as she lightly caressed his hand.

"Jasper, go outside and get some breakfast. I need to speak to General Mil alone." The boy gave her a pouty look, but he hesitantly withdrew. Mil almost felt bad for him, it did seem like he had little say when it came to Anita.

"General, I think you should know that while you were sick, your second was going up and rallying all the men. Talking about how inexperienced you were. And I know it isn't my place, but I would like to give some advice."

No. He knew Bolios was mad at him, but surely Bolios wouldn't actively try to start a mutiny while he was sick? He remembered all the times they had spent together, or the bullies they had fought off. Bolios wouldn't abandon that, would he? But he needed to hear Anita out.

"I think you should find another second. Any second that won't support their general in such a trying time isn't going to be a loyal one."

Mil shot up at the suggestion, and he stared at Anita. Part of him knew she was right, but the other balked at the suggestion. He couldn't simply sideline Bolios like that. But for right now, the pain in his head was getting the better of him.

"Please, go join Jasper, Anita. I need some time alone to rest."

Anita's lips curved like she wanted to say more, but she relented, pulling Jasper up as the two walked out of the tent, leaving him alone to ponder everything.

CHAPTER 17

ARIEL

Ariel wanted to sink into her seat. Over the loud booms of the arguing nobles, and her fathers silent, yet loud stare, she really only could watch as the fight grew and grew. Sweat dripped off her skin as a heap of stress pressed into her chest, but she brushed it off.

Many days had passed since she was first announced to her suitors. Of course, she didn't get to interact with them, but she did see them. An image was hardly enough, though. How was she meant to choose her husband on that alone?

But being publicly announced wasn't the only change. Her father determined she needed to come with him to every meeting. It didn't matter if it was on the matters of state, or something as simple as a dispute between two nobles.

It should have been fine, after all, she was preparing for this her entire life. Yet, it bothered her. How the men looked at her, how they yelled, or even how they didn't look at her.

She was the princess after all, and she commanded power in this room. More than these nobles may, especially with their petty display, one more befitting of children than grown men.

"The Purists are a threat! Why can none of you see that? It won't be long before they decide to annex more territories, or worse! They wouldn't be so inactive unless they were planning something!"

"Please, you think the Purists of all people are a threat? They are merely a band of hooligans. To think you would dare suggest such insolence could topple the crown!" Another one of them retorted back, and at this, her father finally spoke.

"Enough! I will not have arguments commence in my own chamber!" It was rather late, considering the argument had already gone on for a while at this point, but it caused the both of them to pause.

"Although, Sir Danter is correct. We dwarf the Purists in size, and if they think because they took one or two towns they can beat us, then they will be sorely mistaken."

The first noble's face scowled, his nose tightening as he bit right back. "Then why didn't you act when Fieldmoor was taken? Dozens were killed because of their sick games, and even now, you sit back and do nothing!"

Everyone turned to look at the man who said it, eyes wide and jaws dropped. Nobody spoke to the king that way, not even the nobles. Much less a disgraced noble like one from Fieldmoor.

A wad of anger burned through Ariel, furious that he would speak to her father in such a way. But with it, so did doubt. It wasn't that she disagreed that action should be taken, she simply avoided discussing it.

"You dare speak to the King like that?" She lashed out, rising from her chair, letting out an aura of confidence. *A shame it wasn't real.* "If you had a concern, you should have addressed it properly. Not yelled out like a child!"

But when she said it, the man looked not at her, but at her father. His stare was resolute, fire burning beneath it, and at that he sat down. Ariel could tell it was unwilling, but that wasn't what bothered her. He looked to her father for approval, not her, the one who was speaking? Wasn't she the princess?

"You can tell yourself that."

Ariel jolted as she sat back down, a few of the nobles giving her strange looks as she tried to gather herself again. Ever since the nobles party, she'd been hearing that voice, always at the worst times as well.

So she did the only thing she could, ignored it, pretending it was as much a dream as anything else. *You know that isn't true though.*

A heavy aura seemed to crowd them as nobody made any move to speak, until her father spoke up. "Now, what other news is there to share?" There was a bite to his tone that made half of the nobles flinch, but one went to grab a scroll placed on his lap.

"My scouts found a group of armed trespassers, carrying this scroll, sir. I thought it would do better in your hands than mine." Her father grabbed the scroll, unraveling it as she leaned over to look as well.

The parchment was of a high quality, certainly nothing a peasant would be carrying around, but the words were what made her raise an eyebrow.

"We must gather them now. Any more delays will cause it to shift once more. We already have a lead on two of them, the others can't be far."

Ariel didn't know what to make of the letter, and looked to her father, but his face had already fallen pale. "This is a Purist scroll." He dropped it onto the table, one hand stroking his beard as the other was put to rest.

"What were Purists doing so far inland on your territory? They shouldn't have even gotten past the border!" A smug grin grew on the Fieldmoor noble, while this one was now sputtering trying to look for an excuse.

Ariel was at a loss for what this could mean. Were the Purists searching for somebody? But who? And why right in their kingdom? From the stories she heard, the Purists were ruthless zealots, and the thought of them being in the territory sent shivers down her spine.

"Don't be afraid. Even the strongest of humans can crack."

Her eyes narrowed in on the table in front of her, and suddenly, her vision cracked. The scene in front of her fled away, and she was standing on an ashen rock. Smoke bellowed behind her, and she had to resist the urge to cough.

She dragged her hands up to her face, and was met by a mixture of ash and blood. A hideous concoction. Her hair was dragged down into a messy braid, and any makeup that may have been present was gone.

She wasn't wearing a gown either, but a blood stained tunic that had a sword strapped to it. Everything about the vision was wrong. But also right.

"No longer playing princess, heh?"

Her head snapped up, and she saw the scene that was in front of her. A giant temple was at the center of the battlefield, and pieces of it were crumbling and exposed. It may have looked beautiful once, but now it looked like a ruin.

Soldiers surrounded the entrance, some wearing golden cloaks and others dressed in a suit of armor. Bodies littered the ground, along with fallen weapons and blood. Some of the bodies weren't soldiers though, but children too.

"For the Queen!"

A soldier yelled before launching himself into a crowd of soldiers, screaming and blood spatter following. His limp body got thrown out of the huddle, blood gushing out of a crack in his armor.

Everyone was locked into the battle, their concentration unwavering, until a roar broke across the sky. It changed its pitch, the ears ringing trying to comprehend it. It was like no sound any animal could ever make.

Soldiers stopped mid-fight to look up at its source, and the clouds parted above. Rain poured down from their black forms, but they were no match for the creature that emerged from them. A giant creature, dragon-like, but with wings at the creature's front instead appeared.

It was as big as a noble's house, and even the temple looked average when put next to it. The fighting paused for a moment to observe the creature, and a crackling came from its throat. Flesh turned black on its throat and its maw parted.

Lightning escaped out from the beast, shooting right into the temple. People screamed as the electricity ravaged their body, and the temple fell down beneath its weight. A pile of debris was all that remained of half of it, with a coating of arms and blood to decorate it.

At that, the armored soldiers ran forward, screaming victory and yelling as the creature glided down, coming to a landing on top of the broken building. Now she could clearly see, there was somebody riding it, but just as the shadows parted, her gaze snapped away.

"Now is not the time. But soon enough, little princess."

She snapped up from the dream, and at the same time the doors to the meeting room burst open, and a courtier ran in followed by two guards. "Sire! We have urgent news to bring to you." He bowed down on one knee, and the nobles all turned their attention to him.

Her father took in the courtier, and Ariel couldn't tell if he was perturbed or angry at that moment. But he nodded, "Speak, share what news you bring to us."

"A party of guards found a Purist on Evalkyr territory. They managed to capture this one alive, sire. He is being held in the dungeons for further questioning."

Ariel didn't get a chance to process the information before everyone in the room was up and talking over each other.

CHAPTER 18

NEMONA

Her cold breath filled the hallway, the only sign to her figure. The rest of her hid in the shadows, letting the cloak and darkness consume her. Another figure moved in the darkness, but this one was behind a row of iron bars.

Unlike her, he was decorated in yellow robes that were muddied and torn, the light they would have projected stomped upon. There were no guards present at the cell, leaving it a lonely place. Even the other cells near him were empty.

She took a step forward, and his head snapped around, eyes lingering. Something wavered behind them, something not human. An allure, an illusion. Whatever it was, she felt her hair stand up on edge, like a rabbit pinned by a wolf.

"I see even the rats have come to visit me now." He clung his hands to the bars, letting them slip down with an irritating squeal. His hair was not kept, instead wild and tangled. She wasn't surprised. When the guards did come, they liked to break apart the perfect Purist.

"Not a rat." She came out from the shadows fully, letting her hands drop as she stared back at the man. Her blank face wasn't a threat, but it wasn't meant to be a welcome either. She had a reason for being there, and she intended to get answers for once.

"I see no difference. Come now, have you come to ask me questions? Who I am? What I'm doing here? By all means, allow me to sate your curiosities. I am but an open book."

No. Something wasn't right. Nobody gave answers willingly. Nobody gave attention willingly. Why would a Purist of all people give her either? She wavered for a moment, her posture falling as she wobbled, but she snapped back.

Now was not the time to let herself get distracted.

"Who are you, then? What are you doing here?"

He let out a giggle, curling up as he sat against the bars. "I am Maran, disciple of Trisha, and soon enough, I'll be her next apprentice." The words meant little to Nemona, although the name Trisha rang in her ears. She may not know of the Purists ranks, but of course she knew of their commander.

"As for why I am here, it is to do you a favor. I simply wish to cleanse this city and make it pure again. Something anyone should wish for."

Nemona knew what purity and cleansing meant to the Purist, and it was not something she wanted. She had heard tales of how they would drive swords through friendly passerbys, or worse, they would string them up in a line and force their family to watch as they beheaded them. She didn't even know how they got away calling it purity.

"This far into the city? None of your activities would pose a threat to my citizens, would it?"

The Purist turned to her again, giving her the eye. "Your citizens? Do you own them? My, I didn't mean to disturb your property, rat. But as for my activities, that is for me to know and you to figure out."

Her eyebrow twitched at the teasing, but she forced her face to stay rigid. "They are my people to protect, not to own. But as for you, you said you were an open book. Are you, or are you not?"

"Very observant, very good. You truly took me at my word?"

No. She didn't, but the fact he had to lie about it only made it worse. Why withhold some answers and not others? But she had one more card up her sleeve.

"I have another question for you."

"Oh?"

"Why did your group harm that defenseless boy? He did nothing to you."

His smile dropped, and his hands clenched together. "You must be mistaken. I harm no people, and certainly not innocent children."

"You did. He had a limp in his leg, short-cut hair. I know you have to remember him."

Nemona didn't know what she was expecting, but a strangled yell as he turned and slammed his body into the bars was not it. His fists slammed against the metal, bruises forming from the sheer force he was hitting it with.

"You dare refer to the plague as an innocent child? You dare allow such vile words to fill out of your mouth, and touch my ears? That beast could barely even walk."

"He is a child, and nothing you say will change that. You aren't on Purist lands anymore."

"That creature does not deserve to walk this earth! He does not deserve life, much less the title of child. To think you Evalkyr scum would defend it shows you are just as guilty!"

Nemona paused, before furling her hands back and letting them loosen her hood, letting it fall to the ground. "I never denied that I was scum. But if I am, then so are you."

The Purist froze, looking her up and down before breaking out into bitter laughter. "Oh I should have known, why else would a teenage girl come here to question me? To think the king sends his own daughters to do his dirty work."

The word *daughter* hit her like a spear. She didn't mutter any words to him, only staring him down. He didn't know as much as he flaunted.

"I would say thank you for this, but I don't think you'd appreciate it."

Nemona turned, letting her cloak drift behind her as she returned up the steps, the ringing laughter of the Purist chasing her out. After one encounter with him, she decided she wouldn't want to go back anytime soon. But, with how he talked, she wanted to warn the "plague" she knew in town.

She still didn't know if she should have come here. But she felt she had to. Her father would never tell her what the Purists were really doing. The only way for her to find out was to talk to him personally, even if she still shivered from his words.

She knew she wasn't the true princess. Everyone had made that abundantly clear, but she knew she still had more power than most. If the common folk feared the Purists, she would use what little power she had to ease that.

Plus, she had a feeling he wasn't going to stop, even if he was in prison.

—

He stretched up, reaching into his pocket to grab a crystal as he looked back, making sure the girl had left. Oh, what a fool she was, thinking she understood the situation. She knew nothing of what was to come.

He tapped the crystal once, and it lit up, the blurry makings of a face forming on it, like a ripple in the water. "My lord, can you hear me?"

A distorted whisper came through it, and he took it as a positive sign. She most certainly could hear him, and he was close to completing his task.

"The castle will soon be ready for your arrival."

CHAPTER 19

"Ah yes, the fallen disciple. She was a disciple of Commander Trisha, a powerful and sharp-spoken woman, who all thought would succeed the commander. But after a plague hunt, she disappeared. The Purists tried to search for her, but to no avail, and at last, presumed her dead."

- The Purist, Tome I

ALYX

The wilderness, like it always had, served Alyx well. Every passing day was different than the last, but also the same. She would go out into the woods and hunt, then come back to the cabin, where she was greeted like a guest.

She didn't know what to make of it entirely. She had grown so used to being alone, that it was almost strange talking to people on a daily basis. What was weirder, however, was not being afraid of whatever was lurking over her shoulder.

For the first few days, she was sure the Purists would come in the middle of the night. But they never came, just as the old woman had assured her. She hadn't believed a safe haven could exist, but was she wrong that whole time?

She didn't know, so she always pondered it, especially now, when she was tugging her day's catch back. She had managed to catch a stag by surprise, and the animal fell soon after. This forest, she found, was not as welcoming as the former ones.

Where she would usually find open paths and ways, this one was completely forested over. To get anywhere, you had to walk with the plants, not against them, so she had learned to drape her catches over the leaves and pull them with.

When she reached the end of her path at last, she came back to the valley with the cabin, and this time, the little girl waited for her. Nora, who treated Alyx like she'd known her from birth, "You're back!"

She hopped to Alyx's side, looking at the kill with stars in her eyes. Alyx never understood where the sense of admiration came from. After all, at best, she was only a hunter.

"Nora, I already told you, don't dirty the kill!" Nora only seemed to laugh more as she patted it down, as if it was some game. Regardless, Alyx couldn't help but crack a smile at the child's enthusiasm.

"Now, what are you two doing back here? Muddying up in the shadows?" Nora stopped playing right away, jumping away and almost falling to attention. The old woman gave Alyx a nod, before huffing.

"Did you two really expect me to drag this kill all the way up the hill? Goodness, the youth these days." Alyx never could tell when the woman was joking, so she decided to take everything seriously.

She started yanking the stag once again, her arms aching as she dragged it up the hill to the cabin, the old woman and Nora walking beside her. Even now, despite the time she had spent, she knew very little about her companions.

She didn't even know the woman's name, and Nora wanted to play, not talk. She had never pried, because she didn't want to test her hosts, but curiosity did nag at her head. After all, why would she be so kind to a plague-born?

The woman soon took the stag from her, and she settled herself at the table, playing with her hands as 'dinner' was prepared. Nora retreated to her room, not waiting to watch. Alyx couldn't blame her, she didn't much like the cramped cabin rooms.

But where else was she meant to go? Now that she was in a house, she decided she didn't want to return to the wild quite as easily. She let her eyes wander to the woman, who seemed to have an innate focus on her meal.

She was a unique person, for sure. Alyx had learned that she had the leadership of a soldier, and even a Purist would be quaking in their boots if she gave an order. Despite that, for all Alyx could tell, she really was just a shop keep. But, she also had a sense of kindness, and she looked at the 'plague' like she would anyone else.

"Where did you learn to cook?"

The woman paused, narrowing her eyes. "You could say my mentors taught me." She paused, snorting, "Cooking is something anyone should know. Even you, girl." Alyx didn't feel deterred, and the answer only raked more questions at her head.

"Who were your mentors? Your parents?"

She huffed, "Curious, aren't you?" Alyx didn't respond, hoping to still get some sort of response. After all, the woman was the only one she could really talk to in the house.

"You'd know them, probably. They were famous, in more ways than one." Alyx didn't know many people that were considered famous. Perhaps she wasn't very well-read, but nothing rang out right away. "But who were they?"

Finally, the woman swung around to give her a glare, clearly not enjoying this as much as she was. Alyx froze, and the woman recalled her look, shaking her head.

"For your own sake, I wouldn't ask so many questions if I were you, girl. But if you must know, her name was Trisha. And I, Elksie, was her apprentice."

Trisha. Alyx knew that name. Of course she knew that name. It was one of the Purists. And she was her apprentice. She shot up, trying to grab the nearest item to her, her body turning rigid as stone.

"Oh, simmer down won't you? If I was a Purist, you'd be gone already. But even I won't take disrespect in my own home."

"Why should I trust you? You didn't tell me you had connections to the Purists!"

"Hardly. Now sit back down, girl, and we can talk like adults. Not pout like children."

The woman came back to the table, smoke billowing from where she once was as the deer cooked. She fell back into the seat, looking at her in the eyes.

"Like any ol' acolyte, I didn't get a choice to join them. And they fed me lies about what the Purists were. But it wasn't long before that dream faded."

"So you killed innocents in their name?!"

The woman scoffed, "Hold your tongue! Let me finish before you mouth off, won't you?" Alyx obliged, but she pulled her arms back, hugging herself and rocking as she listened, her legs already trying to move, to run.

"I was only twenty when I went on my first hunt. I thought it was going to be glorious, my way into the further ranks of the Purists. And Trisha? She said I was her best pupil. All the stacks were in my favor, but then I saw our first target."

The woman paused, and for the first time, Alyx saw something deeper than annoyance on her face. Her face drooped, and her eyes fell, as if the words were a wave upon her mind.

"She was about your age. Young, but frail. But she was beautiful. A shame none of the other Purists saw that."

Now her head hung low, and a tear made its way down. But her voice still stood strong.

"They wanted me to kill her, but I couldn't. So Trisha got out her sword, and she cut her throat. She was dead within seconds. That's when I knew that whatever fate was to give me, being a Purist wasn't it."

Alyx was dumbfounded. She thought, no, *knew*, that Purists couldn't feel empathy. They killed whoever was in their way, but this woman, she sounded remorseful. Guilty even.

"And you, girl? I'm no fool. The Purists wouldn't be chasing you down like this if you were just any plague. Got something to hide?"

No. She was wrong. They did this to all plagues, she was just unlucky enough to have been seen by them.

"I have nothing to hide! They destroyed my home, and they've been chasing me ever since! There's no reason, they're just monsters!"

Alyx hadn't meant to yell, but now she felt a fresh wave of emotion coming over her, and her throat welled up. Water welled, and then it fell as her cheeks puffed.

"Now, girl-." The woman rose, her hand reaching over, but Alyx slapped it away. She couldn't even get a word out as she was out the door, running towards the woods.

When she looked back, the woman and Nora were standing there, turning into little more than blurs as she ran. She didn't even know what she was running from, other than maybe, the sting in her chest.

Chapter 20

Mil

The town hadn't been what Mil was expecting. The front gates were worn beyond repair, and imagining the inside of the city caused him to shiver. A silence hung over his party as he approached the front stand, where a plump man sat.

"General Mil of the Purists, at your service. We are here due to word of plague inhabiting this town." The man spat out his drink as his head shot up, and sweat ran from his forehead. "Why of course, ya can get free entry!"

The man yanked on a contraption behind him, trying to let the shadows engulf him. Anita came up behind him, and the two exchanged a look as the man began to stutter out. "Ay, what's the holdup? Aren't ya gonna go in?"

"You're the gatekeeper here?"

The man started by nodding his head, before vigorously shaking it back and forth, "Well, yes but I'm only one of many! Working here part-time is its own gig, you know? I actually prefer to work at the bar just downtown!"

Mil was struck by the man's language. Was he afraid of him? Why would he be? The Purists didn't harm civilians. "Would you perhaps be able to direct us? We had reports of a plagueborn in

129

the town. Pure white hair, red eyes, no older than her 20s. Seen anyone like it?"

"No sir! Nobody of that sort got through here. Can't miss somebody like that." This must have been the way the plagueborn got in. The only other way would be through the guard hatches, or climbing the wall. And how could a plagueborn possibly pull that off?

"Well, thank you sir. You know where to go if you do see anybody like that." Mil held his arm up for the rest of the troop to follow as he made his way in, and he had to stop himself from gasping. The roads of the city were rugged, and their carts nearly flew off of it.

But what truly struck him was the people. Shop-owners lined the way, but their stands were held up by sticks, and their forms were skinny and ragged. A few wealthy merchants may have stood out, but the rest looked as if they were at death's door already.

For the size of the city, the guards were absent as well. He watched as a band of juveniles pillaged a fruit stand, while the owner hid in a pile of boxes. Nobody moved a finger to help. How could nobody have known about this? Or even allowed this to happen?

He heard Anita gulp beside him, and at last his eyes landed on something. A girl, no older than five was manning a stand by herself, with a collection of hides and fruits being on display. Only an idiot would leave a girl like that out in this kind of a city.

Without further consideration, Mil went over to the girl, some of his band freezing while others followed. As soon as they got closer, the girl withdrew, drawing her arms around herself. "Why are you here alone? Shouldn't your parents be with you?"

"Mama will be back soon." Mil's eyes softened a bit, but concern still ran through him as he saw the girls state. She may not have been starving, but her ribs were clear.

"Anita, give me one of the rations."

As soon as he got it, he tore the packaging off and handed it to the girl. She held back, but after a moment, grabbed the beef inside and began to tear away at it, like she hadn't eaten in a month. "Why isn't your 'mama' here with you?"

"She's out searching." The girl got out between bites, seeming more interested in her food than anything Mil had to say.

"Searching? For what?" Mil hoped it was food, otherwise he may have to give a stern warning to her parents.

"Big sis." Mil's chest welled up at that, as he could only guess what the girl meant. Perhaps her sister had gotten lost, or had been on the wrong side of the border. Mil had a job to do, but perhaps he could help her after.

"What happened to your sister? Did you see anything?"

The girl shook her head, "She ran off. Ma made her mad I think…" So a runaway? That kind of behavior could get somebody killed in these woods.

Mil frowned when he heard a few grumbles from behind him, his men pacing in the roadway. "And what did your sister look like?"

The girl mumbled to herself, as if thinking, "Well, she had really pretty hair! Like snow! And she had really light eyes."

Mil froze, and his brain started to compute what he told her. It couldn't be, could it? He opened his mouth to ask more, but a figure ducked out from behind the tent. It was an old woman, and she looked at him with the rage of a fire.

"What do you think you're doing here, boy? Trying to disturb my daughter? You can see there is no plague here, so shoo! We don't need your business."

Mil was stunned silent by the ferocity of the woman, and despite him being the only one armed, he backed away, his hands raised in surrender. The old woman didn't lighten her gaze as he left, and watched him until he was back in his troop.

"What was that about?" It was Anita, and Mil wasn't sure what to say. He had found his first lead, yet he wasn't sure if he should pursue it. *What about the job? You can't report back empty-handed.*

"I think I know where the plagueborn might be."

"You do? Where?" Mil let out a deep breath, collecting himself. He would be doing the girl a favor if anything, if her big sister was actually a plagueborn. "That girl was related to it. She said it must have run into the forest. That old woman and it had an argument or something like that."

"That woman? She would harbor a plagueborn?" Mil shrugged, "She may not know. But either way, it's not with them anymore." Anita looked back to where they came from, "Then we should go back to them. They'll be able to tell us more."

"No!" Mil turned around, glaring at Anita, who pulled herself back, her eyes large. "We are not going to involve children in our quest. We have more than enough resources to find the plagueborn on our own."

Plus, Mil already knew something, and that was where the plagueborn must be. If it went into the forest, then it should still be there. There wouldn't be another town in miles for it to sneak to. He had all the information he needed. And part of him didn't want to face the wrath of that woman again, even thinking about it made him shiver.

"Men!" Mil called out, and threw his head down, "We've located the plagueborn. It has been hiding in the forest, and we will track it down from there. Am I understood?" A cry rang out from the men as they fell into order, and Mil trudged onward.

—

When they made it outside the city walls, they were at once stopped from going any further. The forest was thick, with vines blocking their every move, and mud spreading out on the ground.

Mil tugged at Jasper's cloak, the boy gritting his teeth, his feet beginning to drag out of the mud. With one final pull, he came undone, and Mil was left to look at his party around him. Everyone was disorientated, mud covering their cloaks or thorns being stuck in their skin.

They all looked at him, expecting him to handle the problem for them, but what was he meant to do? It would take them days to manually get through the forest, and the plagueborn would hear them from a mile away.

But then, it clicked in his head. "Anita! Do we still have the charges?" Anita dug through the cart, before pulling out what looked like a small ball and stick, tossing it to Mil. Mil let his fingers run over the match, watching as it lit into a small fire.

He threw the match at the ball, then tossed it into the forest ahead. A boom sounded out, and Mil fell to his feet, his head shooting up as he heard a roaring around him. Orange danced in his view, as that small fire soon grew into something greater.

Branches fell, wood withered to ash, and the forest started to break. Mil pushed himself up, moving forward with caution. As the fire burned forward, it also blazed a path, leaving only a thick layer of ash when it had eaten everything else up.

"This way! Don't veer into the fire!" Mil led the charge, members of the party drawing their weapons as they moved forward. Mil felt a sense of relief, because one way or another, they would save the town. No plague would touch it ever again.

CHAPTER 21

ARIEL

The breeze flicked across her hands, but she held strong, even as her body began to ache from the cold. Her eyes were too transfixed by what was in front of her on the balcony, a statue weaving itself, as if in the middle of a motion.

A single runestone was in front of it, a name carved onto its front. *Queen Kossia, of the 15th Dynasty. Let her soul rest eternally.* An ache in her chest began to creep upwards, and she realized why she never liked to come here.

She had her own dreams, of how things might have been different. Whenever she had a hard day, she could crawl to her mother and get a hug in return. Or she could confess her problems, anything, really.

Instead she would always be sitting beneath her father, a cold face looking forward at all that may come. She knew he cared, but he was the king, and she was his heir. There were things beyond parenthood that bound them.

So she was left here, speaking to a ghost. "Mother," She wasn't sure how to start, or even what to say.

"As if it matters. Nobody will hear you."

She bit down on her tongue and finally loosened it.

"I don't know what to do anymore. I didn't think to worry about it, but now I'm not so sure. These Purists- they're monsters! Zealots! I've heard what they do to our towns, how they slaughter innocents. And now they're coming closer to us."

What was she going to do if they attacked the capitol? What if the castle was invaded? How would she protect herself, Nemona? Father, even. She might have been the princess, but she could hardly use a sword.

"Father thinks that they won't give us any trouble. But what if he's wrong? What are we going to do if they attack more villages? I don't know how to handle it! Would we give aid, or attack the Purists? Or would we do something else entirely?"

There was no response of course, but Ariel felt lighter. She only wished mother might be there to say something. *Oh Ariel, you're the heir. You'll know what to do. Just give it time.* How nice it would have been to hear those words.

She gave a passing glance at the statue again, before turning to leave. *"Going so soon? We were just starting to connect."* She froze, a chill running up her spine as she looked back. There was nothing there, but the statue looking down at her.

No. This wasn't happening to her.

Her fists clenched, and she tried to build up anger, something to light her voice on fire. "I can hear you, you know. You can't just ignore me! Who are you? And what are you doing here?"

There wasn't any sign of a presence. She thought the statue might move, or even a shadow would appear, but nothing. A voice came nonetheless.

"Ignore you? Of course not, little one. If anything, I've been the one that's been stood up. It seems you're finally coming around, though." She swore a chuckle followed, but it came from nowhere.

She curled her fists together. She felt like she was a lamb being hunted by a wolf. But this wolf devoured her pain like it was sweets.

"Answer me! I'm the heir to Evalkyr, and I asked you a question!"

The wind let out a howl in response, and a gust hit her torso. Her legs spiraled back as she hit the marble floor, and a sting of pain shot through her back.

"Perhaps we should make one thing clear, dear. I bow to no one, but with you," The voice paused, "I believe we can find some common ground."

Ariel was about to mouth out a reply, but before she could, the door shot open. "Ariel?" Her eyes bulged out as she pulled herself up, realizing at once who the owner of the voice was.

The ki- her father, stood in the doorway, his lips pulled back and eyes wide. "Father." She brushed herself off, standing in position as if she was a soldier, not a princess.

"What are you doing out here? And alone no less?" He came out onto the balcony, gazing at the statue that was behind her. His eyes softened, and he nodded. "Ah. Is this why?"

She couldn't bring herself to admit it, so she only nodded. A pang came to her chest at the admission, as if she had just been cornered. *A princess must have no weaknesses.*

"She was a lovely woman. The best one, in fact, and an even better wife. She adored you." His voice cracked, but he shook it off, "But even to us, life is not always fair."

"What happened?" She had never asked the question before, but now she felt a new wave of courage to do it.

"A sickness. It came on after the birth, and she only lasted for a few years after." He gave her a bitter smile, "Even as the most powerful man in the kingdom, I'm still powerless to nature's whims."

"But you're the king." The king was admitting weakness? That was impossible. If anyone had this power, then it would be him.

"Yes. I am. We're above many- the Purists, peasants, hunger, but we're not above everything." He turned to her then, placing a hand on her shoulder.

"Remember Ariel, being a Queen will not always be about winning. You will win more than anyone else in the land, but you will still lose. And those losses will be what hit the hardest."

"But what kind of losses? What if I lose somebody, or I don't even get the throne? Then what?" That couldn't happen. If she was queen, she would make sure they'd all be safe, but if anything could happen... what if she never became queen to begin with?

"Don't be silly, Ariel. I can't predict the future, but you will be queen. Nobody else has a claim to the throne, and no noble is foolish enough to disrupt our dynasty. Once you are, you will simply have to take the losses as they come."

"How did you do it?" She asked, "After she died, how did you just move on? You never stopped being the king."

"I never moved on." He straightened up, now focusing on the statue once more. "And I wanted to at first, to give up the crown, but it wasn't all sorrow. The greatest thing happened to me that day, and that was you."

Ariel was taken aback by the confession, trying to make sure she heard it right. Her fathers greatest gift, was her? Not his privilege or wealth, but her?

"You only need to focus on the positives, Ariel. For every loss that happens, somebody will stand by you, and that person will be your anchor. Even when one anchor dies, another will come."

"Get inside soon, Ariel. It's getting dark out, and I'll be needing you tomorrow." He took his leave then, and Ariel watched as the final bits of his robe disappeared behind the door. She was alone. Again.

Nothing he told her made sense. How could she be the queen, yet fear death at every corner? And what was she meant to do once he passed? Then who would she have?

You knew it. The whole time. Of course she did. She wouldn't become queen while her father was still alive, but had she ever really thought about it? How could that be her life? Her loved ones dying, and her having no control?

"You do have control. You just don't want to admit it." It was back again. This time though, she wasn't quite as mad at it.

"What do you mean? Of course I could. I'd be the queen after all." She didn't believe the words, but she spat them out like she was rehearsing a play.

"Being the queen won't protect your loved ones. But you know what will? Making yourself a place in this world. Everybody will know not to cross you, Queen Ariel, lest they risk their lives."

"You're sick." Fear her? Why would she want anyone to fear her? She was their queen, not their tyrant. "As if I would ever do something like that. I'm here to serve my subjects!"

"You'll see soon enough. Your subjects don't care the least about you. They'd have your head on a pike in moments."

"Get out of my head!" She stormed off, her shoes clicking together as she rammed into the door to get in. A spree of laughing shot off in her head, and she had to resist clutching it.

None of the servants dared to peek as she stormed to her room, looking less like a princess, but more like an unraveled mess.

CHAPTER 22

ALYX

The mud splashed beneath her feet as she trudged on. Alyx had found that even after living in the forest for weeks now, it still was a mystery to her. It was nothing like the forest she used to live in. She had nothing but the tunic on her back to bring, but it at least made her trek easier.

She had gotten into the routine of walking, and not thinking about how she got into that position. She ignored Elkise and Nora, stuffing them into a box at the back of her mind instead. Her emotions had already died down, and she dared not look back at them.

It was only a matter of time before her feet slid, and her face planted into the mud below, almost enough to hide her white hair. Her fists clenched as she dug herself up, her mind awakening from its haze at the stinging pain in her cheeks.

"Kritz!" She slammed her hands against the ground before pushing herself up, but something else caught her attention. A putrid smell in the air, and one that filled up her lungs as she broke out into a coughing fit.

She had only smelled it a few times before. Smoke. Her eyes flew around wildly, before she finally caught sight of its source. Smoke bellowed up deeper inside the forest, and crackles rang out. *A fire? But it only rained a few days ago.*

But that wasn't the greatest of her worries. The fire was creeping forward, right into the heart of the forest, where Elkise and Nora were. "Drat!" Her previous worries leaving her, she charged forward, the trees flying behind her as she pushed her legs harder and harder.

When she finally threw herself through the canopy, she found herself at the back edge of the house, and her face paled immediately. A long fire drew breath at the front, threatening to eat up the meadow entirely.

From it, however, dozens of shapes drew, the first being a man, who all the others followed. All she had to do was see their garments, and her blood went cold. Purists had found them, even here. But she wasn't going to run. Not this time.

Her hands latched onto the nearest window, and with a few bangs, it shattered outwardly. She grit her teeth as a few glass fragments embedded into her, but her mind was too focused to stop now. She clambered into the house, which seemed the exact same as she left it.

"Nora!" There was no response, so she kept screaming it, even as her lungs waxed. It was only when she heard a small sniffle, coming from inside a barrel that she turned. "Nora?" She pulled the lid up, and curled into a small ball was a sniffling girl.

"Alyx?" She pulled herself up, leaping at Alyx, who had to scramble to catch her. "You're back! I knew you would be!" Alyx felt a leap in her heart, but she couldn't focus on this. Not right now.

"What's going on? What are you doing here?" She returned to sniffling, as if brought out of her little happy moment. "Mama told me to hide until she got me. Said that some 'bad men' are coming."

Well that was an understatement, and not only bad, but dangerous. "Where is she now? You two need to get out of here." Nora shook her head, "She said she'd be back soon."

She couldn't have possibly left now, not with Purists banging on their door. Alyx felt her body heat as stress rang through her veins, and she pulled Nora towards her. Either way, they needed to get out.

"Follow me, and don't make a sound, alright?" Alyx lifted the girl onto her shoulders, gripping her hands tightly as she moved out the window she broke. More glass embedded into her shoulder, but she only bared it, even as tears welled in her eyes.

But now, it wasn't a crackling fire that took up her ears, but the shouts and screams of Purists. Alyx dared a look around the cabin's corner, and her eyes nearly popped out.

Elksie stood at the front of the field, a fallen Purist bleeding onto the ground beneath her. In her hand was a silver blade, and the rest of the Purists hung back, as if they were too terrified to engage.

"Mama!" Nora buckled from her back, charging out onto the field without a second thought. "Nora!" Alyx screamed, darting after her, her hands yanking onto the girl's collar and pulling her back.

"There!" A purist shouted, and the group's attention shifted to her as she wrangled Nora into her arms. Nora only continued to wail 'mama', while cries of 'plague' rang out among the Purists, and Elksie finally turned to look at her.

"You should have stayed gone, girl." She then turned to the Purists, "Get the fuck off my land, you fools!" Despite being outnumbered nearly one to five, she began to approach the group, her sword raised and ready.

Alyx didn't need further instruction. She knew what the Purists were, and there were only two options with them. Run, or hide. She tightened her grip on Nora as she sprinted away, the wind rushing by her.

The forest grew nearer with every moment, and once she was in, it would protect her. "Stop it! Don't let it get away!" She heard screams behind her, but from who, she wasn't sure. She tucked Nora beneath her shoulder, blocking her vision.

She tried to put on a brave face, but her heart pounded in fear. These many purists, right by a forest, and the house. The world seemed to flash around her, the ground was stained by blood, the screams rang out, and the meadow had transformed into a village. *No. No!*

"Watch out!" The whisper transformed into a screech in her ear, and her head flew around, yet a moment too late. Her legs buckled as something hard hit them, and as she tried to struggle, it was as if they were clamped in place.

Nora cried against her, and she tried to use her body to shield her as shadows neared her fallen form. The forest was only a few feet away, but still, too far. "I got it, General!"

The man of before stepped forward, but he seemed to freeze. The two of them were left in a staring match, Alyx scowling her face, teeth bared, as if she was a cornered animal.

More Purists came from the left, three of them restraining Elksie. Despite the woman's old age, she was a force to be reckoned with. *Yet not strong enough.* "Unhand me, you mongrels!"

Alyx's eyes widened as she saw what Elksie was doing. Her free hand reached down into her pocket, and from it came a sharpened piece of silver. Alyx tried to speak to her, hoping she'd see it in her eyes. *Don't. They'll kill you. Don't.*

"Quiet down, you crone-." The Purist was cut off as the silver hit his face, blood gushing out. He let out a scream, and the other two jumped back.

"Crone? Do you know who I am, acolytes?!"

"I am Elksie! Former Disciple of Commander Trisha. Attack me if you dare, but if you leave now, I may spare you." The three jaws fell open, unable to process what they were being told. Even the man who stood over Alyx seemed unsure of what to do.

Until at last, one of the men made a move forward, and Elksie lunged. From behind, a woman appeared, a sword in her hand. "Elksie! Behind you!" Alyx screeched from the back of her lungs, clawing at the dirt as she tried to kick her legs free.

Elksie swung around, but it was too late. The woman cleaved her with the sword, blood flew, and Elksie fell to the ground, a ragged coughing following. The action seemed to put the others into motion, and a voice emerged in the chaos.

The bearded men lurched forward, but he didn't get any words out. She screamed as Elksie fell, digging her claws into the dirt as she tried to get up. Alas, her legs wouldn't move, and neither would Elksie.

No words were said as the woman creeped over to Alyx, shoving a bit of cloth into her mouth. Alyx had to stop herself from gagging, her teeth desperately trying to bite it in two.

When the wretched murder looked down, his eyes shot open as he saw Nora. He didn't say anything, but Alyx didn't need him to. *Who is she? Why is a girl like her with plague of all people?* He was lucky Alyx couldn't speak, or else she would have tore him in two with her words.

"A girl? You took a girl captive, Mil? She doesn't even look like a plagueborn!" A few others nodded to the statement, but the woman, Anita, stood strong. Alyxs vision went red. They weren't even sure? They did all of this just because they could?

"It doesn't matter. Cut off the plague borns head already." Anita muttered, eyes rolling as if the situation bored her. Bitch. Alyx was going to kill her. But first, Alyx decided she would quite fancy keeping her head.

Some of the men started to approach, swords raised, and Alyx tried to creep back. Her free hand went below her, covering Nora's eyes. Was this how things were going to end for her? After everything?

Suddenly, Mil shot in front of her, and all the men stopped. They stared down their leader, a silent question on their lips.

"Considering the circumstances, we need to bring her alive. The Purist will decide what happens to her." His voice didn't sound as cruel as his words.

The bearded man turned to smirk at Anita, who slanted her jaw. "Very well. I'm sure you're right, General Mil." The sickly sweet tone made Alyx want to squirm.

Things should have ended there, but Anita stepped up again. "I am, however, concerned by your seconds behavior. What second questions his general in the midst of battle?"

A scoff emerged from the bearded man, and the Purists all started to look amongst each other as Anita continued.

"I'm sure Commander Benjamin won't be pleased to hear of this fact. From what I heard, this isn't the first time your second has insulted him."

Silence fell upon them, until Mil looked up at the bearded man. His eyes were heavy, but Alyx saw it for what it was. He felt sad at being questioned surely, rather than anything else.

"I'm sorry, Bolios. But she's right. If the commander hears of this, then what?" Alyx wanted to laugh at the fact they were scared of their own leaders. No wonder the purists were such dogs.

Bolios didn't attempt to defend himself. He only looked between Anita and Mil, before finally letting out a growl and stomping off.

Anita was who spoke first. "We should get going. The sun will set soon." She gave a passing glance to the body next to her.

Alyx tried to bite at Anita, but it fell short by a long run. The woman regarded her like one would a rabid animal, but Alyx couldn't care less. They weren't taking her or Nora, not over her dead body.

"Alright. Load them up." The man began to stroke his arm, turning away from the two of them, nodding to his men. He didn't turn to look at them, even as Alyx let out a muffled scream.

Alyx thrashed and rolled, but three Purists picked her up and threw her into the cart. She tried to kick her bound legs at the barrels in it, and clawed at the wood with her arms.

"God! It's going rabid!" Out of the corner of her eye, she could see other Purists approaching Nora just around the body of Elksie, and she flipped over, trying to pull herself out of the cart.

Her blood soaked it, the glass only digging in further, staining her clothes. "Knock it out already! We can't bring it to Commander Benjamin like this. It wouldn't last a day."

Alyx let out a final furious scream, before the hilt of a sword came down on her head. Pain shot through it, but she didn't go out right away. Her vision blurred, but she could still hear the crying of Nora in the back of her head.

"Let her go!" She got out, trying to squirm again, but only being met by another blow. She didn't know how many it took to take her out, but she did remember another few thumping pains, before at last, her vision went black.

Chapter 23

Mil

Mil walked, one foot in front of the other, without another thought. He had been given his big break- a plague hunt, so why did he feel so empty inside? They were only a few more miles from the temple at this point, and he knew he'd be praised.

The plague would be handled, and the child would get an education, food, water, anything you could name. But that only was the tip of his feelings. Was that woman really a plagueborn? Whenever he looked at her, no matter how hard he tried, all he could see was a terrified girl.

The little girl hadn't talked to him the whole ride. She'd only cried out, saying 'mama' over and over, and looking for her 'sister'. They hadn't let the two meet since they took them, and Mil had decided that was a mercy considering what state the woman was in. But that didn't make him feel any better.

That wasn't even mentioning the comrades he'd lost during the mission. Petunia and Lagas, both dead, under his command. There was also the injury Kalt sustained. How was it that he stood there and couldn't do anything? How many more times would that happen?

He found himself repeating a phrase he hadn't in a long time. *Service is absolute and purity is final.* He hadn't had to remind himself, but now he was, because all he really wanted to do was walk into the forest and disappear. He didn't want to present this, and admit he caused so much suffering.

Even some of his own party had been looking differently at him, and he was sure Bolios was at the head of that. Maybe he was right too. How was he meant to know? Everything had become so complex. From guarding the border to whatever this mess is.

"We're at the bridge, General!" Anita called, and Mil let his gaze wander up. On the top of the mountain, a golden and iron temple sat strong, a large symbol of the sun sitting on top. It was the place he was recruited, and where all the most important members of the Purists resided.

"Proceed on." He was listless, and watched as the ground turned from gravel, to dirt, and finally to path again as they came to the impasse. It was only when they got to the final jump that he called out, "Halt!", and moved to the back of the marching line.

At the very end, a tied up woman was sprawled out in the cart, and only a bit in front of her, two Purists rode with the child. She wasn't restrained, but with the way her head dipped low and her eyes welled up, she didn't look like a very happy recruit.

The woman seemed to never sleep, and she was bound on both her feet and arms with ropes, her mouth gagged as well. She looked at him with the eyes of a viper, her fury clear without any words. She probably hated him. And he couldn't blame her.

He didn't know why he came down now, it wasn't as if he had any words. There wasn't anything he could say that would fix what he'd done. So he trudged the whole way back, preparing himself for what was going to happen. He was going home, finally, and he was going to see the Purist again. But with a lot more questions than answers.

The temple's front moved steadily closer to them, when he could finally make out the figures. Numerous disciples circled a man, who he had to guess was Commander Benjamin. The disciples spread out as they approached, their spears planted on the ground.

"Commander." Mil had to hide his frown as he bowed to his superior, who glowered into him like he was an ant. *Maybe he was.*

"I assume you've completed your assignment? You have the plagueborns' head?"

Mil waved his arm out, and Anita followed by Jasper emerged. Behind them, a cart was tugged forward, and their captive lay on it. Her face was scowled beyond recognition, but her body froze when she saw the Commander. *Strange.*

Benjamin scoffed, "Alive? I believe I was very clear on wanting its head."

Mil wanted to argue at first, but he forced himself to ignore the remark. "There's more, sir."

Two of his men led the girl out, who hung her shoulders limp and had her head tilted down. "We found her on our search. She's the sister of the plague, I believe, sir."

"Then kill it as well. The Purists have no use for the blood of plague." Mil froze, his veins going cold. Benjamin wanted him to kill her? She was barely five, if that.

"Now, there's no need to be hasty." From behind him, a cloaked woman appeared, and Mil's eyes widened. It was the Purist, who seemed to be wearing the exact same attire as she did when they first met.

"Purist." Benjamin bowed his head, although his face had the slightest of twitches as he did so. No. He wouldn't dare do that to the Purist, surely.

"Commander." She nodded to him, then turned to Mil, "General, it is good to see you again. I see you've brought someone with you from your travels."

Brought? More like kidnapped. He had to quell some of the sickness he felt at that thought, shaking his head ever slightly.

"Yes, Purist. We have collected a plague and their blood, but there's more."

"Oh?"

"She said she was Elksie, former disciple of Commander Trisha. She attacked us, and we had no other choice but to… remove her. But not only that, the child called her her mother."

"Don't lie to yourself. Open your eyes."

Mil had too many thoughts swirling through his head at once. His disgust was becoming hard to hide, his doubt even harder, and now a voice? He tried his best to ignore it all, pretending as if nothing had changed.

The Purist's shoulders slumped as she shook her head, "Ah. Elksie. I remember her, so many decades ago. A spitfire, but even the brightest of flames burn out with time. She will be mourned for the Purist she once was."

Decades ago? Surely the Purist couldn't be that old, if anything, he seemed older than her at this point. But his attention was drawn away when a loud kick sounded behind him.

He swiveled, and the woman had managed to draw herself up, using her bound hands to claw at the wood as her legs flew around wildly. *Please. Not now.*

"As you can see, Purist, this plague clearly is far too gone. It will only cause us harm if we keep it alive any longer."

The Purist patted Benjamin on the shoulder, "My dear Benjamin, something I still try to teach you- to see opportunity where you least expect it. This plague may be too far gone, but can you not see it? The spirit? It can serve other goals."

Benjamin looked as if he was about to implode, but he only stood there. The Purist then turned her attention to the girl, who bundled up as she approached.

She grabbed at her cheek, and the girl let out a cry as she threw her hands up. "Now, now. This is quite a fine specimen, Mil." She reached down to toy her fingers through the girl's golden locks. "Like a beam of light, shining through a dark corridor. A prime Purist in the making, and of the right bloodline too."

She clapped her hands together then, "Yes, I can see it so clearly now. Bring this one to the Maidens, tell them of her promise." She turned to look at the woman. "As for this one, send her to the prisons, and double lock it. I can sense her resolve from even here."

His men were already starting to move at that, two of them herding the girl inside as she only then started to sob again. "Alyx!" He swore she screamed as they brought her in.

Meanwhile, they approached this 'Alyx' like she was a rabid dog, watching as she circled, ready to pounce. Then they piled on her, restraining every limb even though she already was bound.

That didn't stop her from kicking and clawing, but it didn't matter, and she was carried in by her legs and arms. He wondered what she would say if she wasn't gagged.

Would she talk about what despicable beings they were? How they killed a woman, and kidnapped her two spawn? Maybe she would. And maybe she wouldn't be that far off.

"I'm sure you've had a long journey, Mil. Why don't you rest up?"

It sounded nice, being able to sleep in his own bed for once, going to the bathhouse, speaking with his men. But it all seemed to ring differently after everything.

"But once you're done, meet me in my office. I would love to hear your accounts of everything."

Mil was dragged inside by his own legs at that, his brain once again dulled by sensation. He heard the voices of the Purist and Benjamin as he left, and the heavy footsteps of his men behind him.

But he only let himself be carried to his room, which now seemed dusted and old. How long has it been? He knew not much time had passed, but it felt like years. He couldn't tell either way, but now he was back.

When he opened the door, nothing was moved. Not his tokens of good luck, or figures given by the Purist. It all was in perfect order, but he was drawn to his bed most of all.

He collapsed onto the sheets, letting a sense of fulfillment wash over him. But beneath that, he felt a storm stirring. One he took delicate care to avoid.

CHAPTER 24

ARIEL

Things had fallen into a boring order at the palace. Her father was always busy with his duties, and she was left alone to toy with her own mind. Something which had grown less and less appeasing with time.

Part of her wanted to ask to take the next step, to join him whenever he needed to attend a meeting or talk to a noble. But the other part knew he would tell her when she was ready. He always did. *But was she not already?*

She had taken to walking aimlessly through the corridors, waiting for something, anything really to happen. She'd even take that gosh darn voice over nothing at this point.

But her calls seemed answered when she heard the clicking of boots. Nothing a knight or a servant would wear. She pulled herself behind a pillar, looking for the source, and found it right away.

Nemona was there, a cloak covering her back and boots at her feet. She wasn't even wearing a dress, or anything befitting a princess. After another glance, she moved to a tapestry, and pushed it aside, disappearing behind it.

"Huh?" She came out then, and grappled the tapestry away, only to find a dark corridor in front of her. The palace had these?

"Nemona!" She called, racing down the corridor as a sense of anticipation filled her. She rarely got to see her, but she didn't know this was what Nemona got up to in her spare time.

Part of it sounded more exciting than the duties Ariel was given, but a pad of guilt filled her at that. Of course it was more exciting, but it wasn't like it was doing anything for the kingdom. But at the same time, she wasn't being given anything to do.

She had to drag her hand along the walls to keep her balance, with there being hardly any light in the tunnel whatsoever. When light finally began to flood her vision, she saw an open crevice at the end of it.

But outside of it wasn't the palace, but the gates. It was leading outside the palace. She had never gone very far from it, and was always followed by a whole escort of guards. She didn't even know the palace had a way to so easily access the outside.

She fit one leg through, then managed to squeeze her whole body out, her dress not liking the movement. As she got out though, she nearly jumped as a cloaked figure stood on the side of her. Nemona!

Nemona fixed her a stern look, "What are you doing out here? You should be in the palace!" Ariel swore she heard concern on her tone, which only confused her more. Why would Nemona be worried about her? She was the one coming out here, after all!

"She pities you, clearly. The poor princess, out on an adventure? You're out of your element."

She shook her head, perturbed by the voice. Nemona didn't pity her, nobody did! Why would they? Much less her own sister.

"I should be asking you the same thing! You do realize you're a princess, right?" Ariel gave a coy smile to Nemona, but she only seemed to frown at her comment.

Ariel paused to look around, and green meadows surrounded them. Blades of grass that touched up to her ankle, all leading to the town of Evalkyr. She had never seen it like this. She'd only ever seen it from within a carriage.

"Go back through the tunnel. You're needed elsewhere." A stubborn pull went through Ariel. Why was she out there to begin with? And she had to wonder what was outside of the palace.

"Not until you tell me what you're doing out here! You're going to make father worry sick about you." If she did this after all, he'd mobilize the whole guard force to find her. Ariel couldn't let that happen.

Worse, what if Nemona got hurt. What if she really couldn't handle the streets of Evalkyr?

Nemonas face dropped once again, but her tone held steady. "I'm going to the villages. Now, will you please just get back? The servants are probably already looking for you."

The villages? Nemona went to them frequently? Ariel knew about her people, but she never usually visited them, or spoke to them really. What were they like?

Her mind flashed with the glimpses she'd gotten of them. Their clothes were nothing like hers, but they styled their hair in odd ways. Some even had markings on their skin. It was like they were paintings.

"Then I'm coming with you. I've never been to them before, not on my own, anyway." Nemona didn't argue, which surprised her, and only turned to start walking down a path.

Ariel jogged behind her, watching as they passed by the castle's wall, only to be met with an even larger gate. A whole crowd of people flooded into it, some carrying wagons, and others walking by foot.

Nemona pulled her into the crowd, and like a wave, they flooded through the gate, the guards not seeming all that focused on who was entering. Once it dispersed however, her jaw dropped at everything in front of her.

Stone buildings lined the sides, with people openly crafting in the street, and performances taking place by their side. Most people wore a fine tunic, although even she could see how worn they looked with time.

Merchants crowded the stalls, hauling carts full of goods, while shopkeepers turned their noses up to it. The whole city was wondrous, like an extension of the castle itself!

"So this is what you came for!" Ariel understood why Nemona may want to leave sometimes. Being able to watch these performances, or buy a few goods must have been a nice break from the castle routine.

"No." Nemona answered plainly, pulling Ariel further down. The more they went, the performances started to disappear, and instead she was met with thatch and wood houses, held up by rickety support beams.

People flocked to the front of them, busy with labor, and none of them spared a glance as the two girls walked by. Some children sat alone, their eyes transfixed on the ground, and groups of ruffians held their chins high as they marched up and down the street.

What was once a bustling city center, now seemed to be a desolate slum. Nemona stopped at last when she came upon a group of kids, sat about in a circle throwing rocks to each other. Nemona pulled a loaf of bread out, and handed it to the group.

They didn't mutter even a word of thanks, instead grabbing the loaf and tearing it amongst themselves. They didn't acknowledge the two after that, and Nemona took it as her cue to leave. Ariel was dumbfounded by the whole scene.

"What was that? They didn't even thank you for the gift. Do you know them?" Nemona gave her another look, and let out a sigh.

"I'm sure you know about the Purists, Ariel." Ariel's face dropped as a bit of anger came to her at the mere thought of them. They were who was causing father so much trouble, and attacking their cities.

"Of course I do."

"Anyone who survives them comes here. Not that here is much more welcoming." Ariel knew who the Purists hunted. Anyone that was different, not bright, 'weird'. Were those kids a part of that group?

Now that Ariel thought of it, they did seem a bit strange. Some had crooked noses, others crossed eyes, and the worst of them had an awful break in their bone. It didn't look like it was going to heal anytime soon.

"What do you mean? If they're citizens then they're the same as anyone else." Father always talked about that, how his citizens were meant to be treated equally. After all, what made them any different?

"Yeah. You're probably right." Ariel was dumbstruck once again by the sudden admission. How did she go from claiming they were treated unequally to saying they were equal? *That's odd. Nemona didn't always act like that.*

She gasped when she was pulled to the side, and a hand covered her mouth. "Be quiet." It was Nemona, and Ariel's eyes flew around wildly, before landing on what had startled her.

A group of men were surrounding an old woman, who looked far past her prime. Her skin was wrinkled and grizzled with scars, and she held a cane to keep herself up.

"Ay, ya plague! What you doing in our bounds? Bringing 'em right to us, aren't ya!?" The other men let out a huff of affirmation at this, and the lady turned to try and leave.

They responded by spreading out, blocking her route of escape as they continued to taunt her. "Em royals shouldn't have even let you in! What you contributing to our town? Eh, that's right, nothing!"

"Please, I mean ye no harm. I'm a citizen of Evalkyr, been so ever since I was born." The first man laughed, before swinging down, his fist colliding right with the old lady's nose. She fell to the ground, and the men laughed as a few tried to kick her form.

Ariel let out a roar, and broke out of Nemonas hold. "Ariel! Stop it!" But she didn't, instead she ran right up to the group, despite the fact they towered over her with ease.

"Stop it! Leave her alone!" The men turned around, and a few chuckled as they observed the ball of fury that was blaring her fists at them.

"Issue, pumpkin? This place ain't for little girls like you." A few others leered at her, but at the very least, they stopped assaulting the woman.

"The Law of Evalkyr forbids this kind of violence against citizens! Stop this now!" A hearty laugh broke out amongst the group, some cupping their bodies as they bent over.

"Aw look, the little girl read the law. Wonder what she's gunna do about it."

She growled. These punks clearly had no respect for anything but themselves. She needed to teach them a lesson. "I am the princess of Evalkyr, and if I were you, I'd beat it!"

All of them broke into laughter at once. Ariel's face dropped. Why were they laughing about that? She was the princess for crying out loud! Surely even they were smart enough to see that. "You're the princess of Evalkyr, eh? Guess you can clear our debts then?"

"What? Of course not, hey-."

One of them tried to grab for her, and she pivoted back, kicking him as hard as she could. He yelled in response.

"I wouldn't have done that if I were ya!" Nemona rushed over, grabbing her shoulders and pulling her back. "I think there's been a misunderstanding. She was just trying to.. eh, help."

"I'm sure she was, sugar!" The men moved out as Ariel was pulled to her feet, and now she could see the actual danger she was in. Blood dripped on her face, and the men now seemed content to turn their fury to the two girls.

"You know what we do to girls that don't know their place, eh?" Ariel cast a worried gaze to Nemona, who stood in front of her, cloak still on. Ariel knew a lot, but combat was not one of those things.

"Stop! In the name of the king of Evalkyr!" Everyone paused, and the group scattered from their formation. A group of guards approached, and at their head was the king, who carried a sword in his palm.

The men let out a shriek as they ran, but the guards gave chase, and although Ariel didn't bet, she betted on the guards this time. Her father ran towards her, his hands outstretched.

"Ariel! You're bleeding!" Nemona slinked away, falling back to the sidelines as he fussed over her.

"I'm fine, dad, but that old woman! She got attacked!"

They turned to look at the old woman, who was now crinkled up, trying to sit up on the street as blood streaked her forehead. "Don't worry, Ariel, she seems fine."

He turned her away from the woman, although Ariel wanted to spin around and try to give her treatment herself. "What were you doing out here? Away from the castle, and with no guards? I didn't even know until the servants told me you were missing!"

Ariel gulped, "It was just for a bit dad. Nemona and I were exploring, we didn't expect to run into anyone."

His eyes suddenly locked on to Nemona, who had been silent for the whole ordeal. "You took her out here, onto the streets? And with no guards?"

"Father! Stop it!"

Ariel pushed herself back up to the front. "She didn't force me to go. And I was the one that provoked those men."

Their father clenched his jaw, frowning at both of them. "I expected you two to know better. Ariel, you should have told the maids as soon as you saw Nemona leaving. And Nemona, I know you're smart enough to see how stupid this is."

Nemona looked as if she was going to protest, but instead only nodded her head in reply. Ariel didn't like the emotion she saw on her fathers face. "You and I are going to talk at the castle."

He then turned his attention back to her, "I'll have the guards escort you back. You need to be looked at by the healers."

"Aren't you going to talk to me, as well?"

He huffed, "I hope you consider those bruises enough of a lesson."

Ariel didn't get anymore time to protest as two guards pulled her away, and she tried to career her head back to see what happened to the old woman. But with all the ensuing chaos, she could only make out the shapes of her father, and Nemona.

CHAPTER 25

NEMONA

Nemona looked to the desk in front of her, but she didn't dare sit. She kept her posture straight and stood tall, staring at the wad of fury that sat across from her.

He had gone by many names, king, conqueror, loving husband, and to her, father. However, now, he didn't seem to fit any of those roles, for his face was distorted. If a demon could walk among humankind, it would look how he did now.

They held the stare for a while, and he curled up his fist. She knew he wanted her to speak first, but that wasn't something she was willing to give. Nothing she could say would matter, so she may as well not speak at all.

At last, he smashed his fists together on the table, scrunching his nose to look at her. "Where should I even start? You took Ariel outside of the castle, with no guards, knowing that the people out there could do her harm! I know you're not stupid, Nemona. You should have known the risks."

Nemona flexed her gaze down, and she considered not speaking at all, but a nagging question tore at her. "Don't you want to know how I got out of the castle?"

"What?" His anger deflated for a moment, and he let go of the quill he was holding. Until they tightened again, the quill snapping into two beneath his grasp.

"Nemona. That's a topic for a later date. Can't you see what I'm talking to you about? Your sister is hurt! Instead all you're talking about is your escape attempt?"

Nemona felt her chest tear open, and her heart ache in pain. She had gotten used to hearing a lot of things, but the veiled accusation of not loving her sister? Of course she did. She tried to watch over her when she could, always keeping a distance. The king had made it clear they were in different worlds.

"Ariel wanted to go. I figured that since she was a princess, I didn't have the right to argue." She may have been a princess too, but what favor did it grant her? Ariel was the heir, not her.

"And neither of you even considered the dangers of doing so?"

Of course Nemona knew of the dangers. But she had a feeling Ariel didn't. Nothing was ever very real until you experienced it for yourself. A wad of guilt built in her chest.

"I knew the dangers. I believe Ariel did as well." She hoped, anyway.

"You know I leave the castle from time to time. I've been fine, and I had no way of knowing Ariel would get into a fight."

"So you're blaming your sister? How exactly is it her fault that she was assaulted by a band of hooligans? But you're right. You never have been injured before when going out. Yet, when Ariel came, she turned up hurt."

Nemona let the disbelief flood her face as she tried to unravel what he was asking. She knew that at some level, he had to know she was leaving the castle, but the admission stung. He really didn't care.

"I'm not blaming her, and I should have watched her better. Ariel wanted to see Avatross for herself. I figured if I can go without a band of guards, so could she."

The king only worsened his glare. "It doesn't matter if you meant to or not, Nemona. You admit you made a mistake, and now Ariel is hurt because of it. Mistakes can't be taken back."

But Ariel was the heir? Wasn't she meant to make decisions on her own? Nemona just assumed Ariel knew better than to pick a fight with crooks on the street. Even if it was for a good cause.

"Ariel is the heir. She can make her own decisions."

He leaned back in his chair. "You're right, Ariel can. But it is the job of everyone in this castle to protect her. That's your job, Nemona, and you failed."

"What was I meant to do differently? If I could go out, then she should be able to as well."

"You shouldn't have been out to begin with, Nemona. But nevermind that, enough with this deflection. This still is your fault, even if it was a mistake."

She knew she shouldn't have taken Ariel out there, but what would have happened if she refused? Would Ariel listen to her? Would she still be at fault if she didn't? At worst, she made a mistake, and at best, she was only doing what the princess asked. Either way, was it really this serious?

"You'll be staying in your room until I say otherwise. The maids will bring you anything you need."

Her jaw dropped. He was going to restrict her, even more so than Ariel was? He never cared to do something like this before, and he never once brought up how she could be in danger. Would he do the same if Ariel was the one that snuck out?

You already have the answer to that. He didn't punish her at all. Was she really going to take this?

She raised her head to him, and stared at his fiery eyes. "I overlooked something as well, King Xaden." His body tensed at his full title, and much of his anger dropped.

"This whole time I thought there was a reason behind this. Behind why you ignored me, and gave Ariel everything. But now I realize I'm pointless. I have no merit, no worth in your eyes. Do you even love me?"

His eyes morphed into huge circles, but he didn't reply. He didn't let his gaze drop either, or even dare blink as they exchanged glances. She felt lava boil beneath her skin, and she took a step forward.

"Is this what mom would have wanted? She always kept us together. It was you that separated us, you that divided us, and treated us like this."

He stammered, "I don't know what you're talking about. I do love you Nemona. I've made sure the maids looked after you, even if I wasn't around. You and Ariel have always been my priorities." His face caved in on itself, and he struggled to hold himself together. It was then that Nemona knew he was lying.

He turned to look at the large portrait behind him, and it was of mother. She was so beautiful in the picture, immortalized like a goddess. He spared one more look at it, before turning back to her.

"Please leave, Nemona. I need to think."

Nemona knew she could have stayed. She could have sat there and argued, to tell him everything he's done. But what was the point? Would he ever care, would he ever stop to think? Or would he turn into something worse? She already knew what he said wasn't true.

She looked back to the painting of mother once more, and turned out of the room. She didn't dare to look at him again.

CHAPTER 26

ALYX

A growl emerged from her throat as she was thrown against the cell wall, a loud bang following as the cell door closed. She ran up against the bars, her hands clenching on to them, "Let me out, you monsters!"

The two Purists didn't respond, wafting away as soon as she was secure. Her eyes glowered at their backs as they moved away. They had removed her restraints, but considering she was now in a cell, it was hardly a reward.

"Another one?" A voice called from her side, and a few more let out huffs of agreement. Alyx's interest peaked. There were other people here? She thought, no knew, the purists simply killed anyone they met.

"Who's there?" A chorus of responses awaited her, some mocking, others nonsensical, until a final voice silenced them out. "Plague. Like you. Except we're the unlucky kind."

The realization hit her like a truck. The purists took them prisoner? But why? What could they possibly gain from that? She already knew they had no morals.

"What is this place? A slaughterhouse?" Her mind couldn't process her own words as she tried to fiddle with the bars, her fingers picking at the locks, yet to no use.

She knew Nora was inside there somewhere. With the Purists no less, and that fact gave power to her bones. Yet, no matter how much she wanted to break it down, the cell wouldn't budge. The cell was empty, and she had no means of escape. At all.

"Oh, it's far worse than that hun. Just you wait till they come on back." What could be worse than a slaughterhouse? What could be worse than them killing off a whole village?

"Tell me." She pleaded, "What's going on here? Why am I here? I know all they want is to kill us."

"If you're lucky, they'll just feed you a bunch of liquids till your skin is blue and eyes are bulging. If you're not, then let the Ravasts have mercy on you."

Alyx almost wanted to laugh at the bitterness. Calling on that old legend now of all times? Maybe things were starting to get hopeless now. She could handle a swift death, but what about this? Being trapped and tortured until she died? Knowing that Nora was being taught by these monsters.

"So they're here to torture us? When? How?" Heavy footsteps rang out, and the whole cell fell silent. Alyx held onto the bars tighter, her teeth gritting. "I need answers, please."

"Be quiet." A voice whispered, and the torches blew out as a cold breeze entered the cell block. Two shadowy figures entered, their metal clanging against the walls.

They stopped by her cell, and Alyx flew back, clinging to the back wall. The first one opened the door, and she flew forward. Her arms reached for his sword, but before she could, the other slammed his gauntlet onto her head.

The other reached for her cloak, and her head stung as she was yanked up, carried around like a kitten. She tried to scratch against their leggings, but her nails only ripped and tore in response to the harder metal.

"Darn plagues." One of them muttered, which only caused her to tense up more. They pulled her through the block, and into another corridor, where she heard the loud conversations of Purists.

Lights lit up the hall as they dined, distracted, and not witnessing it at all. Her mouth opened at that, and she screamed. The scream startled them all, and they swirled to look at the scene. And she recognized some of them. The very same ones that had kidnapped her.

"Shut her up!" One of the men covered her mouth with his hand, and the metal snapped at her teeth. So she only glared at all the ones dining, who still couldn't get rid of the shock on their face as she was dragged away.

So, only the ones to deal with her were armored. Well, that was reassuring. The halls got bleaker as they moved on, going from golden and silver to granite and stone. She swore a few cracks lined them as well. Human-shaped cracks.

When they reached a door, she was carried in, and slammed against a stone table in the middle. She kicked with her feet and arms, but they only responded by holding one down at a time, pulling straps over her.

She hated it. At least before she could wiggle in rebellion, but now she was a sitting duck. At least she wasn't gagged.

"You're going to regret this!" She seethed, wishing she had a sword, or anything sharp that she could stab right into their figures.

"Yeah, and what are you gonna do about it?" It was the first one, and he had an ear to ear grin plastered on his face. "Get the serum! I wanna hear this one scream."

The third shifted uncomfortably, but the second dipped his head and turned around, rummaging through the nearest shelf.

When he spun around, he held a bowl with a golden liquid in it. It looked like honey, but the smell made her face well up in disgust.

She shut her lips, but the first one grabbed her jaw, pinching it tight enough she yelped. The next thing she knew, a stream of liquid fell into her throat, burning as it went down. Her throat pulled in and she tried to gag it out, but it only kept coming.

When it was finally over, she felt like her throat was on fire, and her head was fuzzy. She tried to speak, but only a few unintelligible murmurs came from her mouth. *What was going on?*

The three figures began to warp, and her hands felt numb and detached. "Now, tell us, what do you know about Elksie? What was your relation to her? And that girl."

Elksie. Nora. The words felt so powerful in her mind, but her body felt limp. She tried to process what she was told. Elksie was a friend. So was Nora. She knew Elksie was a purist once. Then they killed her.

"Hurry up!" The first one shouted, and she felt a sharp tingle in her side and a bang in her ears. She swore she should have been feeling pain, but she didn't feel much of anything. She was trapped, and the prison was her own body.

"Elksie." She got out, trying to focus and figure out what to say. She should trick them, but her thoughts were like a wildfire, and picking them apart was a struggle.

The first one seemed like he was going to scream, but the second one spoke up instead. "Elksie, she's your mother, right? And that girl was your sister."

"Yes." It came out before she could fully grasp what was being said to her. Elksie wasn't her mother! The term mother felt like nothing, and she tried to grasp who that was. There was a face in her mind, but it was so vague.

The three let out gasps of surprise as they muttered amongst themselves. "That couldn't be right! A Purist would never give birth to a plague, and what about the girl? They couldn't be related!"

"It has to be true! Why else would they all be together, and why would Elksie shelter a plague? She was blinded by love! Can't you both see that?"

The first one broke their argument. "It doesn't matter either way. We have what we need out of it. There's no reason to keep it alive."

The third one stammered, "But the Purist had clear orders! We were to keep her- it alive until further notice. She'd have our heads if we disobeyed her!"

"The Purist would never want a plague alive. She just wanted the information out of it, and now we have that."

It hit her suddenly. It was like time slowed, and her vision unfogged. She could watch as the first grabbed a spear from the shelf, twirling it in his hands like it was a toy.

They weren't here to interrogate her. They were trying to kill her. *She was going to die here.* She tried to fight against the restraints more, but they wouldn't budge.

The two looked at each other, "Wasn't the serum meant to last a bit longer? She's already waking up."

The second slung his shoulders, his brows raised. "All the others have been out for hours, even days! I must not have given it the right dosage."

"Enough." It was her voice, she realized. But she wasn't the one speaking. "This game is getting tiring." Her head turned to each of them. "Must, Pare, and Dinger."

The three all froze, the third dropping the spear in shock as it clattered to the ground. "You! How do you know that!? Were you spying?"

He charged up, grabbing at her collar, but she didn't react. Couldn't. "I know far more than that. I know your commander, Benjamin, was not part of the original standing. And I also know about your leader, the Purist. Or should I say, Amasha?"

If they were still before, the three didn't move an inch now, their forms like statues. Alyx didn't know what to do, and she was about ready to scream herself. She was speaking, as if she knew any of this! *What's happening? What's going on?*

"Forget. None of this ever happened." This time, she wasn't speaking, but she could hear the words all the same. It was the last thing she heard before everything fell out, all turning to black.

—

She yanked herself up, her hands clenching against the cold stone floor as her head whipped around. Her cell. She was in her cell.

Her head ached, and she tried to pull on what she remembered. She was here, talking to the prisoner. Purists. Captured. Did she fall asleep? How, in this decrypt thing?

"Amasha." The voice was like a spring song, and Alyx turned to face it. Her face twisted to rage. It was her, the same one at the gate- and the one that took Nora.

"I had forsaken that name long ago. But I suppose it is only fitting that the plague brings it to my doorstep once more."

What was she talking about? Was she mad? *Probably. As if all Purists aren't.* She stood like an animal, waiting to pounce and tear her to shreds. But lucky for her, there was a ring of bars separating them.

"Nothing to say? How curious." Something about the tone felt off. It was still sweet, pleasant, yet behind it, she swore she could hear something. Something sinister.

CHAPTER 27

MIL

Mil sat in the dining hall, Anita by his side, although his eyes were drawn to the empty seat next to her. It was where Jasper would have been sitting. His whole party was letting out jolly laughs, blissfully unaware of their absences. "I can't believe it! The Purist herself welcomed us back! Next thing you know, we'll be reporting to her directly!"

They slammed their glasses of ale together and drank, but Mil let his sit on the table. He wasn't in the mood for fun games, or for drinking himself blind. How could they have shifted so easily? One minute, they're kidnapping two people, and the next it's like the good old days.

"Oh cheer up lad! You're bringing the whole table down." The rest murmured in agreement, and Mil let out a sigh as he grabbed his ale, taking a few sips. He didn't know what the rest of his party thought, and he wasn't so eager to talk about it. Maybe they had the right idea anyway, to move on. It's not like he wasn't aware about what plague hunts were.

"And Anita! Boy, you moved so fast! Next thing I knew, that old witch was on the ground bleeding." A chorus of laughter broke out, and Mil gripped the handle of his mug tightly. Anita gave a light smile in response, something which took him off guard.

170

"It was nothing. She left herself open, after all." Mil was frozen, his jaw hanging open at the remarks. The woman was a former Purist, and one of the highest ranks. Yet they were talking about her like she was scum. Even the Purist complimented her.

"A real shame for that girl, though. Imagine being so unlucky, getting a plague for a sister! She probably didn't understand any of it." Anita continued, and the party nodded in agreement. "Why, if I had a plague as my brother, I'd cut his head off!"

Another of them cut in, "Ay, but did any of you see how Bolios acted? He told off Mil for trying to subdue the plague! Shameful!"

Anita added on, "Indeed. He got what was coming to him with his demotion."

What made it worse was that Bolios and those closest to him were gone. Who knows where they were at, and his party was taking advantage of that to insult them.

More joined in with their criticisms of Bolios, until finally Mil snapped. "Stop it! All of you. I'm sure Bolios had his reasons, but bickering amongst ourselves isn't going to do anything. What's done is done."

Mil couldn't bring himself to regret removing Bolios as his second, but sometimes he had to wonder. Was Bolios right? The woman did look like a plagueborn to him, but she didn't act like one. She tried to protect a child, and she feared them. But at the same time, even the Purist didn't seem to object to her being a plague.

"Fine then, but on that topic, when are ya choosing your next second, Mil? It's a bit overdue at this point!" Mil paused, and the whole table seemed to shift to him with expectant eyes. He'd been too occupied to ponder the question, but it needed to be answered.

Anita was a strong warrior, but what she said today caught him off guard. Jasper had his heart in the right place, but now he was ghosting him. He struggled to think of anyone else that came to mind, or even fit in the role. He needed time to think.

"I'll choose one, but we should all get settled in first. We won't be going out on a mission for a bit. We'll have a second before then." The group seemed satisfied with the answer, but that wasn't what caught his eye.

From the corner of his vision, a young boy garbed in a linen coat approached. A messenger. He stammered as he spoke, "I'm looking for General Mil, sirs."

Mil rose, his mind pondering why a messenger would be looking for him of all things. He could think of more than a few less favorable outcomes. Was Benjamin unsatisfied that they brought the woman alive? If they hadn't, he would have gotten his wish after all.

"The Purist has summoned you. She'd like to speak with you immediately." Muttering broke out amongst the table, and Mil knew why. Everyone knew the Purist watched over him, but they didn't know they were this close.

"Lead the way." It was a nice distraction, and he was glad to get away from the conversation. He missed the days they could talk about their funny slip-ups, or their daily routines. Now it was all about the plague, or their command.

The messenger slipped away, and Mil had to trot to follow, but it sent him reeling to the past. He remembered when he was one as well, and had to run around, always fearing who he might be sending a message to. At least this one only had to fetch him.

As they were walking, a scream suddenly rang out, and he swung around. It was coming from the dining hall, and he heard a few exclamations along with it. What in the griffin's name was going on down there? Was that plague?

"Sir, the Purist insisted on seeing you, and soon." The messenger gulped, and Mil pulled himself back. He didn't want to know what was going on down there, in all honesty.

The messenger led him down the halls, until finally they reached a broad door, and a familiar one at that. A griffin and manticore stood off, painted in ivory and gold. The same place he had the fateful meeting with the Purist. How long ago? Sixteen years now? Time flew by him.

He felt his chest press in as the messenger opened the door, and they walked down the halls. These halls were the place his life got changed for good, and now he was returning to them. For what though, he wasn't sure.

Nothing about the room had changed, and just like before, the Purist sat at her desk, cloaked and her face covered. "Why thank you, Den. You may go now." The messenger dipped his head before scurrying out, and the two were left alone.

"Mil, it has been a while! Alas, I apologize for not being able to catch up sooner, but duty calls. I'm sure you can relate."

"Of course, it's no issue. I'm sure you've been hard at work." He sat down at the nearest chair, and debated what he wanted to say. Things felt different now, very different, from their previous meetings.

"I was quite impressed with your most recent work. Most first plague hunts don't go so well, and you managed to bring back a new acolyte as well! You always were an overachiever, Mil."

The switch, the girl, all of them rang in his head. He had so much to ask, yet so little time to ask it. And part of him wondered if it was a good idea to even bring it up. But what other choice did he have?

"Erm, about that. My whole party was rather confused when our commanders switched, and we were only told by Commander Benjamin. May I ask why?"

The Purist adjusted herself, straightening her posture as she bore into Mil, and he wondered if he'd ask the wrong question for a moment.

"Ah, yes, well I suppose anyone would be. Commander Trisha has other matters she must attend to, so Commander Benjamin will be your commander until she returns."

Good. The change wasn't permanent at least. Mil would never say it out loud, but he would always prefer Trisha over Benjamin, even if he respected them both as commanders.

"That's good to hear. And what about that girl? Has she been doing well?" Mil remembered his acolyte training, and although there were upsides, it was an arduous process. But even he was older than that girl was when he was enlisted.

"The Maidens have been caring for her. There's no need to worry. Perhaps you could even visit sometime- but enough about that. Mil, I've hardly had any chance to ask about you? How have you been? I haven't seen you for months!"

Mil didn't know where to begin. "Well, things were interesting in our last few weeks. I, well." He became a general, he was sent on a plague hunt, then he had a rift in his party and he had to demote Bolios. Bolios, his closest friend.

"Well, Bolios had to step down, and ever since my troop has been divided. Not everyone was ready for the plague hunt, and now I don't know what's going to happen." He let his head fall low, and deep down, he knew he had failed as a General.

The Purist twisted her head, in a gesture that Mil conflated as both empathy, and judgment. She never was one to show her emotions on her face, quite literally.

"Trust your men, Mil. Purists would never turn against each other, although I am sorry to hear that. It must have been awful to go through. And everyone's plague hunt is hard at first, but we get used to it."

"But that isn't the only thing. With that woman- I couldn't see the plague in her. She seemed like anybody else! And you didn't kill her, so I was wondering…" He didn't know what he was asking. Wondering if she was actually being recruited as a Purist? He doubted it. She was probably rotting in their dungeons.

"Ah." The Purist reached over, her gloved hand patting his shoulder before retracting. "The plague often disguise themselves, Mil, it is no surprise it appeared like that to you. I have spared it to tie up some loose ends, but nothing more. I wouldn't concern yourself with it."

Mil reeled back, feeling dejected. His questions didn't feel answered, but dodged. The Purist wouldn't do that though. She was only telling him the hard truth, that was all.

Before he could continue, though, two figures burst through the hall. "Purist! It's about one of the plague! They started speaking nonsense and, oh flaming feathers- they knew our names, and the Commanders status!"

"Slow down, Pare. What is it exactly it told you?" Mil was shocked at how frantic the man seemed, it was like he had seen a ghost.

"It told us our names, then it said that Commander Benjamin was not one of the founders. And it called you- Amasha? Whatever that means."

The Purist went rigid, and so did Mil. What plague told them that? Could it be that woman? It had to, what other plague would they be storing there? But how would she possibly know any of that? And Amasha?

The Purists gaze drifted to her statue, one of a griffin, before nodding and getting up. "Bring it back to its cell. I will meet it there."

"I do apologize for this interruption, Mil, but feel free to make yourself at home. I'll be returning shortly." With that, she was whisked away with the two men, and Mil was left there. Alone. That should have felt enlightening, but if anything, he just felt more unsatisfied.

CHAPTER 28

ARIEL

Ariel felt like she was being pulled in ten different directions as her maids slung her from one station to the next. Her hair was yanked and twisted, and she may have snapped if not for the three brushes in her face at that moment.

"Oh, you're going to look just lovely, dear!" The maids call, and Ariel felt a sinking feeling in her stomach as she stared at herself in the mirror. Her face was dolled up with all sorts of paints, and her hair was pulled back into a fine braid. She looked like a picture really, any picture.

She knew why they were prettying her up like this. She was nearly an adult, and with that came new responsibilities. Like keeping the bloodline in tact. Nausea ran up her throat at that thought, and what would follow it, but what could she do? It was her duty as princess, and she knew what father expected of her.

"Who's in attendance?" She managed to snake the words out, and Bessa burst out laughing.

"Who isn't? This is your joining party, Princess! No noble would dare miss it." Ariel wanted to groan at that. On the bright side, maybe, just maybe, one of them would be acceptable, but she doubted it.

"Now hurry along, princess, we mustn't be late!" Ariel would rather stay in that room, staring into the mirror, but she had no choice in the matter. Her feet were dragged forward by the sea of maids, and she watched as the room vanished, and then the halls flew by her. It was like she was a passenger in her own body.

She could hear the loud booms of voices as she approached, and honed in on one, her father's. "I must thank all of you for being present, and having brought your son's here. This is a momentous day for us all, as we can see the union of two families!"

The nobles cheered in response, and a thought flashed through Ariel's mind. She could leave then, run into the very back of the palace where nobody would find her until the next day. But then what would she do? When she saw fathers disappointed face, glowering down at her.

But did that even matter? He was the one forcing her to do this anyway. Her mind flashed to the last week, where she had gone out with Nemona. He saved her, and yet that look she saw on his face as he observed the old woman. It was all enough to cause her body to feel weak, but to run off?

"At last, let me present, Princess Ariel!" The maids pushed open the door as she stepped out with them. They left her alone as they fanned out, and she was left to see the giant crowd that was in front of her. She was meant to find a suitor out of that many people? In a night? How was that even possible?

She looked to her father, and he rose up, grabbing his chalice as he held it to the ceiling. "Let us commence!" Waiters emerged from the sides, carrying around trays of food that the nobles dined off of at will. They began to form into groups, and she saw just how many members of each family there were. *She was meant to court them? Together? Yuck.*

With a gulp, she walked down onto the base, her head swinging around to see all of the people present. As soon as she made her way down, at least three men all shoved their way in front of her. They bore over her in height, and she swore they looked at least five years older than her.

The first one bowed down, "Why, Princess Ariel- I'm from the house of Rator. Perhaps you would care for a dance?"

The second one butt in, "Ignore my younger brother. We could go get a drink near the bar?" The third one reached over, grabbing her wrist.

They barraged her like a bunch of animals, and she snapped her wrist away. She didn't want to dance with any of them, she wanted them to go away. She glared at the group, pushing her way through as her dress dragged behind her.

She tried to close her ears as more invites got thrown out, and she kept walking. Why wasn't her father helping her? Or even her maids? She was never trained for this, or what to choose. Part of her wished her father had just given her a match already.

The night passed on much like that, and her head started to ache and pound. Men kept barraging her, some who'd already been told no, and at some point, she had resigned to giving dances away like they were candy.

She prayed that it'd be midnight soon, or whenever her father planned to call off this horrid event. Nobody was a good dancer, not as they threw her around like a prop. But she met her match when she was once more caught up with the three of before.

"Princess, I was speaking to your father. We were perhaps thinking of arranging a private courtship? One where there's not so much noise around us." Could he not take no for an answer? Was her ignoring him not clear enough?

But she also had to catch her breath at that idea. Would father really do that? Have this big ceremony then pair her up with one of the least desirable men? She could never let that happen. She wouldn't.

"Then don't. You're the princess. Control them. Control this ball!"

Her hands balled into fists, and she shoved her hands against the first man. "I'd never marry you, you moron! Now leave me alone!" She charged past him, pushing through every guest near her until she was at the very back of the ball. Then, she made for the door.

She shoved out of the room, holding her dress up as she ran through the garden out back. It was a pretty place, with a stream of water, the chirping of insects, and all sorts of plants. But all she cared about was that it was empty, and rid of any of the suitors.

She gripped onto the nearby railing, squeezing it tight. She would have to go back in, and then what? Be punished for pushing that man down? He deserved it anyway. She wished she had Nemona right now, but she had vanished too. *Probably because you got her in trouble.*

She wanted to ask father to make it go away, and let her marry who she wanted and when. But could she bear to see that disappointment? That his only daughter couldn't do what was expected of her? That she, the heir, was too much of a wimp to take one for the kingdom?

She could imagine the scene in her head. *Ariel, first you sneak out of the castle, and now this? You were raised your whole life for this! The kingdom needs you. I need you. You can't keep doing this, not when your duties call!*

"Are you alright?" Ariel spun around, and in the front of the garden was a man. He didn't seem much older than her, with dirty blonde hair that spilled down into his face. His face was drooped, and his eyes sparkled.

"Who are you?" He held his hands up, as if in surrender.

"Cassor Blackfield, ma'am. I assume you're Princess Ariel?" The relief that hit her when he didn't introduce himself with his house. It was like he was a real person, an actual being.

"The balls in there, you know?" He nodded.

"Of course, but I saw you run out. Plus, who would want to go back in there?" She couldn't stifle a giggle at that, because he was right. The ball was a disaster, and she would like to stay away from it.

A glimmer of hope stretched in her chest, and she walked closer to the man, who stood still. It was like she was inspecting him.

"You're going to have to choose a suitor. You may as well choose one that knows how to heel to royals."

That voice again. She had become accustomed to it, and in some way relieved. It always seemed to side with her, but now its advice stunned her. Choose him to marry? She wasn't sure she was ready for that, but maybe it did have a point.

She'd have to choose a suitor sooner or later, and he was the only one she'd found that was even half-decent. And if she waited too long, father may pair her up with somebody.

"Maybe we should go back inside. We could dance?" She tried to give the most innocent look she could, and he only smiled and brought her into a hug.

"Of course! That sounds lovely."

—

181

NEMONA

Nemona crept through the cramped passage, letting her arms glide with the grace of a predator. She didn't let anyone hear the scrapings of stone as her knees pressed forward, or her huffed breathing. She had to get answers.

At last, she heard the voices of people, and stopped right in front of a grate. She poked her head forward, and spied at least five figures in the room. One of them was Cassor, but the others she didn't recognize.

"I assume the princess took your affections well, dear?" A middle aged woman spoke, dressed in the finest of robes. If not for the ugly wrinkles on her face, she would have been a perfect representation of mother.

"Yes, mother. I believe marriage won't be far off."

The oldest member there spoke up, "Then make it soon! We must marry into the royal line. Only then will we reclaim our glory!" The man shifted around, smacking his cane into the ground.

"No nobles will speak poorly of us ever again. Not when we rule the crown!"

Their celebration was cut short by the shrill of Cassors voice. "But, mother, what if she doesn't listen to me? She has quite the temper."

The mother let out a scoff, "Don't worry about it, dear. If Princess Ariel suffers a sudden accident after being coronated, nobody will bat an eye."

Nemonas face didn't waver. Nobles were always the same, but anger took her nonetheless. *How dare they threaten Ariel.* She tucked backwards, and let her view of the grate disappear. She had to warn Ariel.

CHAPTER 29

ALYX

The days had started to blur together for her. The guards no longer came to bother her, and she was left to rot in the cell. Every other day she'd get thrown a stale piece of bread and some stew. She wanted to gag from the smell alone, but she had no choice but to wolf it down.

She'd tried to speak to the other prisoners more, as soon as they started to talk, the guards would rush over, banging their spears against the bars, yelling at them to stop. Alyx didn't know why they were suddenly doing this, but it made conversation virtually impossible.

She tried to think of an escape plan, anyway to get out, but it was a locked box. The bars couldn't be budged, and she knew there was a key to each cell, all held by the armed Purists. If she got taken out again, it may be her only chance to escape, yet they seemed to show no interest in her.

It was the loud blaring of a horn that snapped her out of her thoughts. A line of purists marched into the corridor, one blowing into what looked like a battle horn. "Line up! It's play time." *Play time?* She shivered at what the words could mean.

The guards started with the cells in front of her, before finally coming to hers. She saw a line of prisoners being formed, no

Purists in sight. *They weren't being forced. They were lining up by will.* She moved out into the line, her head snapping around for the nearest escape route.

This could be her chance, yet something still ate at the back of her head. The fact any of her fellow 'plague' would submit to this willingly. She would sooner die than allow them to torture or experiment on her, so why wouldn't they?

The horn blew again and the line started to move forward, with Alyx being forced to keep pace so she wasn't run over. They didn't go out of the gate she had been brought out of, but instead curved into a small passage. There were no windows or ways to see, and whenever she tried to turn back, she was shoved forward.

When light finally flooded through, she was pulled through a door, and her jaw dropped at what she saw. It was a field, fenced in the same way a farmer may a pasture. On one side was the temple they came out of, and on the other, she could see as the mountains rolled out. *Freedom.*

The horn came out again, and she turned to see three Purists, all sat on a balcony overlooking the field. "We thought it only fair to let all plague be immersed in their natural habitat. You all will have the next hour to yourselves."

Despite the message, the purists did not move from their station, and continued to watch the group. Alyx felt a wave of doubt wash through her. These monsters would never do anything nice for them, whether that be outdoor time or even seeing the sun.

She ducked low, moving next to the person nearest to her. It was a younger man, and if she had to guess, he was nearing his fifteenth birthday. His body stuck out like a crude creation, certain parts being much larger than others, but it didn't phase her.

"What's going on?" She hushed, and he smiled in return. "It's playtime! Only time we even get to be on our own out here!"

With that, he moved off to run, like a deer that had been caged for the last year. *That probably hit a bit too close to home.*

"Get down! Get down!" It was like a scream in her ears, and she dropped down, her body rippling. She hadn't heard the voice in a long while, but it had saved her on more occasions than one. As everyone else ran, she hugged the ground like a corpse, her eyes flickering to the purists.

They watched the runners, and began to point at a few. It seemed like they were having some discourse, before finally, they turned and went inside. She looked to the ones they pointed at, all of them were sprinting like dogs, crossing the field in no time.

She didn't know what the pointing meant, but she stayed on the ground for the rest of the hour, even as her legs begged to run. After what felt like days, the horn rang out, and everyone started to line up again to the tunnel. She didn't move, however, staying glued to the ground.

As the group began to walk back in, Purists emerged from the side doors, weapons strapped to their waists as they split up the line. The tunnel door slammed behind them, and any noise that might have been there was drowned out.

"Take them to the back!" The purists jumped then, wrangling the stragglers, all of whom kicked and thrashed. A sinking feeling hit her as she realized who they were. The same ones the purists had made a deal of prior.

She rose then, her heart pounding in her ears as she raced over. She wasn't going to let the purists kill another person in front of her, not again. "Let them go!" She shouted, trying to seem intimidating to the much bulkier Purists.

"Another one?" One of them huffed, going to grab something at his waist, but freezing as another patted him. The other one shook their head, motioning to her before pointing to the tunnel. He reached over at that, his hands going to grab her sides.

She whipped side to side, before finally, hitting her head against his hand. As soon as her teeth touched his skin, she bit and tore. She thought of how she saw wolves attack their prey, even as they still kicked and screamed, but this time, she was the wolf.

The man let out a cry of agony, hitting her head until she slid off and he scooped her up like a plank of wood. The next thing she knew, the tunnel door was open once again, and she was thrown in. She leaped up as soon as she could, banging upon the door, but it wouldn't budge.

She was cut off, unable to hear or see the others, and her gut sank as she imagined what was happening to them. She must have stayed there for a few more minutes, before finally, she turned and walked back through the tunnel.

She cursed the purists and their wicked ways, she cursed all the people that had to die for them, and most of all she cursed their leaders. Her mind became a storm as she pictured the man, his ratty black hair and shaggy beard. He would be the first one that she'd kill.

The tunnel at last opened up into the cell block, and Alyx stepped out into the middle. The purists were strangely absent, and she was left alone. She looked at all the cells around her, some full, but more than a few empty.

With no footsteps ringing out, she creeped up to the front, and peeked into the hallways that spread out. She was taken through the center, and that was where they took her, and where they seemed to eat.

The other two had to lead somewhere else, and one of them had to be the exit. She jumped as she heard the echoes of footsteps, and moved back into the prison. She stalked to her cell, which was still open from when she came out before.

She moved into it, snapping the door back, then pushing it. *Good. It wasn't locked.* She closed the door, and watched as the guards stepped back into view. They paid neither her nor her cell any mind.

If the purists thought she would go down easily, then they were wrong. A plan formed in her mind, and she for once felt powerful as her muscles tensed. She would wait until the guards left, then she'd find out what was down either of the two corridors.

Once she found out where Nora was, and then the exit, she'd just need her chance. *Then they'll pay.*

CHAPTER 30

MIL

The Purist had been too busy to talk to him in the following days. Whenever he was with his men, he felt the looming weight of his decision standing over him. He could only see one person for the job- Anita, but part of him hesitated.

How she cut down that woman, Elksie, who was a former Purist herself. He struggled to look past it, but that was only the start of his worries. Bolios had been avoiding him ever since they made it back. He wanted to talk to him, but he couldn't bring himself to do so.

He knew Bolios didn't want to see him, and as much as Mil wanted to rekindle their connection, he didn't know how. He was a coward, and he didn't deny that. But what was he going to say to Bolios? How was he even going to attempt to explain himself? The answers proved too heavy for him, so he tried to shift his mind away.

Instead, his mind kept wandering back to the plague, and the girl he had captured. His men had told him later it was that plague that caused the scream. He knew taking plague wasn't commonplace, so what would they be doing to her? And where was she?

He may not know on her, but he did on the girl. She was with the Maidens, the same place he had been at her age. He hadn't ever gone back there, not since he became an acolyte and moved to his tutors. He almost felt hesitant to, but curiosity won out.

So he found himself walking down the purist halls, lost in thought as he looked to all the rooms he passed. First, the halls, offices, all places only the most distinguished and known Purists would be. Then there were the barracks, where everyone else was kept.

His favorite place, however, was the library, where every drop of knowledge the purists knew was stored. He could have spent a whole year learning everything there was, and it was one of the many places he missed while away.

But before long, he was face to face with a huge wooden door. It was like a barrier to everything else, as while the walls were plain before it, peering inside, one would see walls patterned with all sorts of shades.

He took in a deep breath, before pushing the door open, walking into the empty hall. A few waiting seats were in an otherwise barren room, with a whole section of doors leading away. He had never been to this part before, although the style made an odd feeling rush through his bones.

He sat down on one of the chairs, twiddling with his thumbs as he waited for someone to arrive. Despite it being where all the young Purists are taught, the room was deathly silent, and everything seemed as if it hadn't been used in years.

"Master Mil? Oh! I almost didn't see you there." A cloaked woman emerged from a side door, looking almost exactly like the Purist. He may have confused the two, if not for the absence of the mask the Purist always wore.

"Maiden." He bowed, observing her form. She did not look much different from the other Maidens he knew, but this one was a mystery to him. "May I ask for your name?"

"Oh of course, sire. I am Maiden Annagreth. Is there any way I may help you? Visitors are so infrequent these days."

"Yes, well, I helped bring in a new Purist, maybe a week back? Her name is Nora. I was wondering how she was adjusting."

Mil tried to rack his memory for how he felt when he was a young Purist, but his memories were faint. He barely remembered anything before his days as an acolyte, although if he tried hard enough, he could see lavish meals and extravagant beds, all better than what he had now.

"Oh Nora! Such a sweetie. She had a hard time at first, but I do believe she's adjusting quite well. Perhaps the presence of a familiar face could help her adjust."

Mil hadn't expected to be invited in, but he found a hard time disagreeing. He was curious about the state of the girl, and about the elusive Maidens, whom nobody would see for long. "I suppose it may. As long as I'm not interrupting anything."

"Of course not, Master Mil! I'm sure the children could enjoy the presence of a Purist. They rarely get to see any, after all. Right this way." She ducked through the side door she emerged from, and Mil followed suit, having to crouch down due to his head almost hitting the doorway.

As the door shut behind him, he could finally make out the delighted giggles of children, their loud voices ringing down the hall. The walls too shifted, looking less like a formal building and more like a playroom. It was probably the most innocent part of the whole temple.

At last, the room revealed itself, and Mil found himself unable to move. A long table sat in the middle, holding an assortment of dishes. Everything from pudding to steaks, but that wasn't what the children were focused on.

Instead, they were playing with all the balls and toys in the room, pushing them between each other. When Mil entered the room, few gave him notice, until Annagreth cleared her throat. "Children, a Master is here. Don't you all remember what to say?"

The children turned then, looking over Mil like he was an exotic animal in a cage. "Welcome, Master." They drilled out, and he was unable to tell if they were interested in him, or only doing as they were taught.

"Now, have any of you seen little Nora? Master here has been looking for her." The children all shrugged and looked amongst themselves, before one finally spoke up, pointing to a pillar at the far corner of the room.

As Mil levied his gaze to it, he saw a small figure hidden in its shadow, clutching something to her chest. Annagreth let out a huff and waddled over, pulling the girl out of hiding. "Nora! You know how rude it is to hide when a Master is present. Now, go ahead and say it."

Nora sniffled as she watched, jumbling her words as she tried to say something similar to 'Welcome, Master'. Annagreth continued to nudge her, until she was only a pile of snot and tears.

"There's really no need. That's more than enough." Annagreth let Nora go, who retreated to the corner, giving a frown in his direction.

"Ah, but the children will never learn if we do not teach them! She must learn with time."

Mil didn't know how to reply, so he went about changing the subject. He decided not to question the Maidens' words, no matter how callous they seemed to be.

"Has she been having a hard time adjusting?" Annagreths face softened, and she paced a bit. "It is to be expected. Her file is quite the interesting one- daughter of a Purist, sister to a plague! I can only imagine what the poor thing had to go through at home."

Of course, that excluded what his men had done, killing Elksie and lighting their home ablaze in front of them. But what grabbed Mil's attention was the mention of a file. He never knew such a thing existed for the children, and figured their pasts were forgotten.

"File? You have a file for each child here?" Annagreth chuckled, "And for every Purist that has ever lived within these walls! We even have one on you."

Mil was taken aback, because in truth, he never had let his mind wander to what he was before the purists. He knew he must have a family, but for all he knew, they abandoned him. And he had lived with the purists his whole life, surely they now filled that hole.

"You have a file on me? Where?"

Annagreth pointed to a back door, "The archives, silly! You could take a peak if you'd like, I'm sure Minevra wouldn't mind."

Minerva. The name rattled in Mil's head, and he saw the face of a middle-aged woman, her hair curly and brown, holding him as she read a story. The rest of the children gathered around, huffing at the fact they weren't being held themselves.

He hadn't thought back to her, not in a long time, but all he could do was nod to Annagreth and march towards the back door. When he opened it up, he was met with tall shelves in every which way, scrolls filling every part of them.

It must have taken hours to sort through all of them, until at last, he found one titled 'Mil'. It had no last name on it like the others, and it was rather small. He opened it up, watching as black ink filled its pages, and it began to tell a tale.

It talked about two farmers, living out near the fishing village of Sansaks. They were an oddity for their time, having no children and not living as the rest of the village.

Miracle must have blessed them when one day, a son was born, and he was going to inherit their small farm when he was of age. Before any of that could happen, however, a band of Purists came seeking inscription when he was a few years old.

They argued that he was too young to be taken, but the Purists disagreed, and took him anyway, along with any other children they could find in the village. That was the story of Mil, and a rather quaint one at that.

Mil closed the scroll, unsure of what he was expecting to read. That his parents were from a long lost dynasty? Or that they were powerful warriors? But no, instead they were simple farmers, and he was taken away from them.

He imagined himself instead of hunting plague, plowing the fields or caring for animals, a sweet, yet simple job. He bit his lip as he went to put the scroll back, before seeing a figure to his left.

The woman in front of him was old, but not in a weak looking way. Her features radiated out, bathing the room around him, and even if her wrinkles deceived her, men must still run to her feet. He recognized her right away. Minerva, but not as soft as he remembered her.

"Mil. It has been a long time." She looked at the scroll he was holding, and her face curled back into a scowl. Mil let his face drop, wondering what the sudden aggression could have come from.

"Reading your own scroll, Mil? What is the meaning of this?" He put his hands up, as despite being nearly twice her size, he felt fear run through him at the woman's tone.

"Maiden Annagreth said I could read it, Maiden Minerva."

Minerva let out a huff as she turned around, slamming her cane against the ground. "Fool." She muttered, "I suppose I will have to talk to Miss Annagreth. What have you read from the scroll, Mil?"

Mil felt pressure in his chest, a part of him not wanting to speak of the farming parents, or how he was to run a farm. So instead, he kept it vague. "Not much. Simply about how I was collected."

She snorted. "Good. Let us keep it that way, and I suggest you cleanse your mind of anything you read today." She pointed towards a door at the far end of the room, "That will lead you back towards your section of the temple."

Mil didn't know how to react to the dismissal, and stood there frozen. She levied him another gaze, and turned, regarding the shelf. "You know, I have heard of your predicament, Mil. I like to keep tabs on all of my past students."

Predicament? Mil didn't know what she was referring to, he had too much to choose from at that point.

"My advice, don't keep your party waiting any longer. You already made one poor decision in a second, don't make another and fail to choose one."

At that, she trotted away, and Mil struggled as he remembered the woman who snuggled him, and now the one who snapped at him, barking orders like he was a dog.

He could have asked more, but right now he only had one question. Why?

CHAPTER 31

ARIEL

"And you're sure about this, Ariel?" Her father's eyes bore into her, but Ariel wasn't intimidated. Instead, her eyes sparkled in response, and like an animal seeing light for the first time, she nodded vigorously.

He mumbled something to himself, but relented, looking to Cassor. "And you wish to engage my daughter?" He stumbled on his words, but managed not to crumble under her father's eye.

"Yes, sir. I could not think of refusing such a generous offer."

Offer? Ariel grimaced at the language, but shook it off. He was only being formal in front of her father, nothing more.

"Well, the courting must go through the proper channels before I can allow it. You are dismissed, Blackfield."

He exited the chamber, the rest of the nobles staring as he did so. Only when he was gone did the shouting erupt, nobles scurrying to speak over each other.

"You can't allow this, my lord! He is of a disgraced lineage. They have no town to call their home. If anything, they mooch off us. And you would let that mooching turn to the crown?"

Another one cut in, "Exactly! Not to mention how dismissive they've been of the crown. Giving a giant statue of a random creature as a gift? How were the royals ever meant to use that?"

His face drooped, and he leaned back, clasping his hands together. "I don't disagree with any of you." Ariel froze, her pulse flashing as she heard her father speak out. "But I will not go against my daughter's wishes. He is still a noble, and hardly that of a peasant."

"Still a noble? The peasants on the street probably own more land than they do! We should have stripped them of their title over a decade ago!"

"Will you let them push you around like that? There's a reason they speak out. They want you to marry them instead. You can't let that happen."

"Enough!" She lashed out, stepping up to the front of the table. "My father has already told you what's going to happen. Are you trying to defy him?"

The nobles paused, and Ariel let a wave of victory wash over her. She hated how the nobles would pester about any little thing, and she never knew how her father tolerated them in any capacity.

"Ariel!" It wasn't a noble this time, but her father. "Sit back down." He turned to look at all the nobles. "All of you, leave. I need to speak to my daughter alone."

The nobles filed out of the room, and Ariel was left facing her father, who descended from his throne. His face was worn, and he looked down to her with something she couldn't fathom. When was the last time he ever showed anything but happiness to her?

"Ariel. The nobles had a point. This Blackfield, he isn't of high standing, and he has a questionable position in court. Ever since Arbornail got taken, his family has been drifting between different refuges."

"You said I could choose any one of the nobles! Now you're limiting it even further?" She already found most of them distasteful, and of course when there was one that was even tolerable, her father had complaints about him.

"I will respect your wishes Ariel, but you need to understand what you're doing! Marriage isn't all about who you love. I got very lucky, but you may not have that chance."

"I'm not going to marry one of those despicable nobles! They'd drive me mad!"

Her father let out a snort, his face scrunching up. "I'm not asking you to Ariel! I'm asking you to look beyond yourself. Consider what effects this marriage could have on the crown, not if you personally like it!"

She let out an angry call, spinning on her heel as she stormed out. Of course he'd do this, why wouldn't he? Make it seem like it's her choice then take it the second she finds someone. It was going to be arranged from the beginning, she bet!

"Ariel! Stop!" She ignored him and flung the gates open, marching out in the direction of her room. She was doomed. She either could marry someone that would 'hurt the crown' or she could live the rest of her life a miserable maiden.

She was going to be the queen, and she couldn't be controlled like this! If even her own father would try to do so, then how could she trust anybody else to not?

"You can't. That's why you have to handle them. Your father can't control you, he's too weak-willed."

For once, she resonated with the voice, and its call to freedom. It was right. She should be handling these people trying to restrict her and trap her. She would never allow herself to be a slave.

Cassor was waiting right outside, and he let his head fall down, toying with his fingers. When he saw her approach, his head snapped up, but a smile didn't form on it. "What did the king say?"

"My father." Ariel corrected, not especially pleased with giving compliments to 'the king' today. "He said that he'd 'allow' the marriage, but made a point of talking about how unfavorable it was! I can't believe he'd try to limit me like this."

Cassor let out a sigh of relief, and shook his head. "Well, I'm sure it doesn't matter. You'll be queen soon enough anyway, and then his decisions won't matter. Plus, I'll be the new king alongside you!"

Ariel was still furious at her father, but not so mad she wanted to look at his death like it was a good thing. Her mind flashed back to the empty room she saw as a child, and she stepped back from Cassor.

His face dropped and he stammered, "I didn't mean anything by it Ariel. Your father is a good king- the best in fact. I only meant you shouldn't worry. He'll come around with time, I bet the news is just a shock to him."

"Yeah. You're probably right."

Ariel leaned into his chest, and he responded by wrapping his arms around her head. Just as she was relaxing into it, her eyes caught something pop out from behind a hallway. It was a gloved hand, and it motioned for her to follow. *Nemona?*

She wanted to remain there in Cassor's chest, but she hadn't spoken to her sister after they snuck out. Another thing to get mad at her father for. "I'll be right back, Cassor."

She withdrew from his chest, and he called out, "Ariel? Wait!", but she didn't stop, and continued her way down the hall.

There she saw Nemona, cloaked in a dark vest, holding a lantern in her right hand. She didn't look like someone who would be wandering the castle halls. Ariel went to ask her what she was doing there, but Nemona spoke first.

"So you're getting married." Oh great. Back to this. Her body went rigid, and her fists curled up as she went right up to Nemona.

"And so what if I am? It's not any of your business!"

Nemona didn't react to her aggression, and kept a straight face throughout.

"Be careful, Ariel. The nobles aren't looking to marry you for anything other than power. And once you marry, they'll be the one in control."

She was right about the nobles, but Cassor was different! His family had been disgraced, and he knew not to get on his high horse or manipulate her. She could just tell.

"Cassor wouldn't do that! He'd let me rule as queen. You don't even know him like I do."

"No. But I know his family."

More of this? How many times was she going to have to hear how they were a disgraced family, losing Arbornail to the purists? She was so sick of it.

"For the last time, him being from a disgraced family doesn't mean anything! They'll build up their prestige again after we marry! I can't believe you would be preaching this too, Nemona!"

"I don't mean that, Ariel. Wait!"

Ariel didn't listen as she continued marching away. Her whole family was against her on this, and for what? Her father didn't have to go through this, and Nemona sure as hell didn't.

She guessed she was the unlucky one, forced to suffer through this thanks to whoever's whims. But it wouldn't be like this for long. Things would change. For now, she needed to get back to Cassor, the only one who listened at this point.

"Oh, much sooner than you may think, little one."

CHAPTER 32

MIL

Mil hadn't expected to be summoned to the Purist again, especially after his encounter with Minerva. He had never feared the Purists' wrath, but now he did. He could only imagine what Minerva may have said about him behind his back.

The boy is undisciplined, sneaking into our archives, stealing his own files. Punishment must be wrought.

He shivered from the mere thought, especially as he creaked forward to the familiar hallway. The painted door no longer interested him, and as he stepped into the hallway, neither did the passage. The same things that brought him wonder as a boy now acted as dull reminders. Even he wasn't so far gone to realize that was wrong.

As soon as he put one foot over the threshold, he was frozen at what he saw. What was once a beautiful array of trinkets and gold was now a mess. The bookshelves were unorderly, books taken and tossed about, some open on the desk, others on the floor.

Anything that sat upon those bookcases was either broken or gone, and the only things in the office that remained untouched were the Purist's desk and the griffin statue. The Purist sat by the desk, palms pressing into a book. Her grip was so hard the pages were pressing in on themselves.

When she saw him, her gaze snapped up, and she seemed about to attack him before pausing. Mil was starting to wonder if the woman in front of him was the Purist, but when she spoke, all his doubts were quelled.

"Mil." She rasped, adjusting to a more comfortable position, and making sure to shuffle her desk to at least resemble something orderly. "I summoned you here with good news. After considering your performance in the plague hunt, it is only customary that I promote you."

His jaw must have hit the floor. He was only made General at most a month ago, and now he was being promoted again? He didn't deserve that, and it would be against every code! The Purist must have known what she was doing, but what if he really wasn't ready? What if he failed?

"From now on, you'll be a Premier General, and be able to lead expeditions without the permission or supervision of a Commander. However, with the position comes information."

Mil couldn't let this go on any longer. If he was given even a drop of this information, he would have to be a Premier General, and he couldn't be. He already knew how worthy he was. A murderer didn't need any more power beneath him.

He let the word sink in, because deep down he knew it was true. You're a murderer. You let an old woman be killed, and your actions led to that 'plagues' death as well.

"I can't." The Purist snapped her head up, interrupted from her speech by the mere words. I was only promoted a month ago, and nothing I've done marks me as worthy of a promotion."

The scathing look the Purist shot him made him want to jump back. Never had she looked at him with anything other than perhaps interest and joy, but everything about today seemed off for her.

"Mil, I appreciate the concern," Her tone didn't match what the words wished to convey, "But I know who is worthy of being a Premier General. My pupil, you are more than worthy, and anyone else that disagrees is clearly not versed in the ways of the purists."

"But, please, you have to understand, I'm not ready-."

Her hand clenched and she spoke, "Mil, I will not discuss this any further. You will be a Premier General. Do you understand?"

He wanted to keep listing off the reasons he shouldn't be, and in an ideal world, she'd have listened. But he knew now that she wouldn't, and deep down, some part of him didn't want to disappoint her.

That feeling only deepened as he recounted her words. *Pupil.* The Purist, the highest figure in the purists considered him her pupil. He was somebody that would go down in history, but did he really want that? To be known for that?

"Nobody should hear what you say today. If you tell anyone, they must be approved by me. This information is not for any Purist to know."

Mil nodded, and his mind circled on what would be so valuable nobody else could know. He always had thought of the Purists as an open book, but clearly, that assumption had been broken more than once.

"There are more reasons than purity for killing plague, Mil."

Mil could feel his mind crash against his skull as those words were said. *What other reason could there be? He'd been taught his whole life purity was the only reason.* Everytime they would curse the plague for purity, it'd be for a different purpose?

"I'm sure you heard of the myth of the Ravasts, Mil?"

Of course Mil had, after all, the legend was famous, but he didn't understand how it applied here.

"I have been searching for the Ravasts all my life, and yet I've only ever been able to find one. If we were able to get all of them, Mil, we could purify the entire word."

Mil had to hold in a cough as she kept speaking. The Purist really believed in those fairytales? And furthermore, he had been killing plague over them? Would they even purify the world?

"But then, why haven't we been searching for them more? All we do is hunt plague!" He was leaning forward now, his fingers drumming against his sides. He didn't know what it meant, but something about him jumped in joy at that fact.

"You must understand, Mil, this information is too important for just anyone to know. The plague are still a threat, and killing them is nothing to scoff at."

Mil zoned out as the Purist began to talk about all the tales of the Ravasts. Some were completely ridiculous, such as one king claiming a Ravast came to his doorstep to give him a golden crown. Others had more truth to them, but either way, Mil didn't see how it was important.

"Now that you know this, we can get on to the matter at hand. I'm sending you and your party to the Ashtuk Mountains. I believe a Ravast may be there, and if we have two, we'll be one step closer to defeating the plague."

"A Ravast? How do you know one is there?" Even if there was a Ravast, how would he possibly capture it? If they were as powerful as the Purist said, wouldn't it just kill him and his men?

"I have my ways. All you need to do is follow this map. If you can't find it in a week, then you are to return at once and report. Now, follow me, I will need to announce your departure."

The Purist rose from her seat and made her way back out to the hall, and Mil followed her. He wasn't sure where they were going, but his mind was still lost in their conversation. There was a plague farm? And he was going to the mountains, to find a relic of mass destruction?

Part of him wondered why it was always him, but the other feared something greater. What was he doing? Once he was killing plague for a noble cause, now he was killing them to try and track down some kind of fairytale?

He tailed the Purist, weaving out of the way of various Purists as they made a hurried pace to the auditorium. Usually, the Purist always had a slow and steady pace, but now, Mil had to jog to keep up with her.

As they passed into the room, she carelessly flung her hand against the bell, ringing going about as she made her way onto the stage. Mil went to take the seat closest to him, but stopped when he heard a clicking noise. He looked up, and the Purist shook her head, pointing to one of the front seats.

Mil had the full weight of his new role hit him as he walked all the way up, sitting down at the front. Before, he had only seen people like Monbek sit here. *Monbek. What would he think about this? About Mil being in this role?* His heart fell as he thought about the rift between him and Bolios, and the face Monbek would make when he heard.

At that point, crowds began to flood in, and more than a few spared a glance to him sitting in the front rows. Still, nobody said a word, and it only took a few more minutes for the auditorium to be overflowing with Purists.

He glanced behind him, and spied his crew- Anita, Jasper, Bolios, and so many more all sitting in a row. Anita smiled back at him, while Bolios only frowned as Jasper watched on.

"My dear Purists, I have news for you all today. A young Purist has shown his potential to me, and will be awarded accordingly." She shifted her gaze to Mil, and he squirmed as he felt everyone's eyes land on him.

"Mil, for your acts of bravery, you will be promoted to a Premier General. With this new role, your squadron will be sent out to the Ashtuk Mountains."

Murmurs didn't break out among the purists, but Mil could swear he heard mental ones. Nobody would dare interrupt the Purist, but surely they had to wonder. Why would he of all people be a Premier General?

The Purist rattled on a few more orders for other squadrons, but none that he knew, before waving everyone away and dismissing them with a flick of her wrist.

Mil hadn't noticed before how much power she commanded. He watched as full crowds, including himself, wandered out of that building, all with the motion of her hands. *Was that who he was going to be? A ruler?*

He felt a bit sick to his stomach at the thought, but he snapped up when he saw someone approaching him out of the corner of his eye. He twirled around, expecting to see Bolios, or worse, Benjamin, but his heart lightened when he saw who it was.

Anita was there, and followed by the whole squadron. They all kept a good two feet of distance from him, as if segregating themselves. "I was pleased to hear your decision, Premier General Mil. Thank you for choosing me as your second."

What? He hadn't chosen anyone for his second. He had considered Anita to be the best option, but he hadn't done anything. He froze as he replayed the words Minerva had told him in the weeks prior. *You already made one poor decision in a second, don't make another and fail to choose one.*

Anita continued to smile up at him like a new puppy, and it hit Mil. Just like his promotion, the choice had been made for him. It made sense suddenly. He may have been a Premier General, but he still was the acolyte that wasn't trusted with his own decisions. Somehow, he had been made to straddle that fine line.

"Anita." He bit out, "I need to talk to you. Privately, it's uh, about the mission." Anita tilted her head, a flash of something else coming over her, before she fell back to the warm smile of before.

"Of course, Premier General."

The two shimmied farther away, but he had to spare a few glances to make sure nobody was listening in. "You can't repeat this to anyone else, but…" He trailed off, wondering if he was making the right choice. He was defying what the Purist told him to do. *But with only one person?*

"The Purist doesn't only want to kill plague. She wants to find the Ravasts as well."

Anitas face went through a flurry of different emotions as she processed the news, but he was sure she wasn't the source of the increasing yell he heard. He only had a few moments to step back before Bolios was hurtling at him.

They skidded to a stop, and Bolios let out a scream. "Are you kidding me Mil? We've been going on missions to kill plague, all while the higher ups have been chasing down ghosts?"

Jasper moved up behind him, "You weren't going to tell us? At all? Mil, aren't we deserving of knowing what's going on behind the scenes?"

"I couldn't! I wasn't even meant to tell Anita. I don't like any of it either, but-."

Bolios cut in, "But what Mil? You were going to hide it for them? Does that make you any better?"

Anita jumped in front of Bolios, despite the fact she was almost half his size. "You should be ashamed, speaking to your Premier General that way." Her gaze snapped to Jasper, and he stumbled back, his eyes welling with shock.

"I will speak to him however I want, Anita! We were the same rank only a month ago. If you aren't going to question him, then I will."

Bolios charged forward, pushing past Anita, but froze when a new voice filled the hallway. "Is something wrong, boys?" Everyone turned, and Mil went still as well.

Commander Benjamin scowled his face as he looked on at them, and most everyone dipped their head right away, chanting out, "Greetings, Commander.", or something of the like.

Bolios lowered his fist, and paused, looking between Benjamin and Mil. "No, nothing's wrong sir." The words were sharp, and Mil had a good feeling Bolios meant none of them.

Benjamin only gave a sneer as he walked by, "Let's hope that's true then. If it wasn't, I wouldn't know what to do first. Demote the incompetent general standing before me, or execute the lot of you for your mouthiness."

Nobody moved a muscle as he walked by, and they all stood like that until Anita spoke up. "Should we depart then, Premier General?"

Mil wandered his head for the right response, still trying to snap back from the threats the general made. They should have left, considering the Purist wanted it done soon, but he had one more thing he had to do.

"Soon. There's something I need to do first- please take everyone to the front of the temple for me, Anita."

With that, he turned and sped off, heart thumping as he ran through the halls. He may not be able to get answers, but maybe, just maybe, he could get closure.

CHAPTER 33

ALYX

Alyx never knew how hard sitting still could be. Escape was right in front of her, but she had to ignore it if she wanted to get Nora and leave alive.

She tried to keep her gaze away from the door, because she knew with just one push, it would fly open. There were guards at each end of the hallway, four more than before. If she tried to run now, she would be caught.

In her mind's eye, she could see meadows unfolding, trees with strong roots, and animals that hunted through it all. She saw the forest she had been in ever since she was a girl, and every creature that had helped her survive.

She remembered the first raven she watched crack open a nut, or the wolf that tricked its prey into running into its pack. The wilds had much to teach, and she had gulped up all of it. However, the most important lesson she learned was from a grizzly.

The grizzly had been injured, bite marks placed on its leg, and it had been calling out. For what, she wasn't sure, but she swore she could feel the pain that radiated off its tone. She was still young, and her hiding spot didn't obscure her from the bear's gaze.

It stared at her for a long while, and she stared back, too afraid to move even an inch. It was so big, that with one swipe it could have smashed all the bones in her body. Despite this, the bear looked at her a moment longer, then turned around and left.

Her mind flashed back to the present, and she let it all resonate within her. She needed to wait for the time to strike, even if her heart burned with rage ready to consume every Purist that stood there.

That thought was cut off when footsteps rang out through the marble floors. She looked up, as did every Purist that was stationed there, and a man emerged in the hallway.

He was decked out in a sickeningly fancy robe, and his hair had been well trimmed and kept. He should have been a spitting image of the purists, but as her gaze focused in on his face, he looked too normal to be a part of them. Her eyes flashed, and her fingers scratched against the floor. She knew this man.

"General Mil, it is an honor to see you. How can we be of service?" Alyx had to withhold a gag at the suck up of a man. She'd bet everything he didn't actually care about this 'general', he just wanted to look good.

Mil looked around at the quarters, his eyes wide and jaw dropped. The man intervened right away, stammering out a sentence, "I know it can be quite a shock! So much scum surrounding us, you're brave for even coming here."

The general's jaw tightened, and he shook his head. "Yes. I just didn't know that you- we kept the plague." The man didn't seem to know how to take this, and let out a laugh.

"Well, it's nothing to worry about! We'll make sure none of them ever get out."

Mil nodded his head, and turned to look right at Alyx. Alyx bore her teeth and scowled her face, snapping at him wildly. The cell may have been utterly despicable, but even then, she took comfort in knowing it was hers, devoid of any Purist scum.

"May I have a moment alone with her? I would understand if not, however-."

The general didn't get a chance to finish as the men were already booking it down, yelling a string of words, "Of course! Of course! Why, you didn't even need to ask!"

Did everyone in this place wait hand and foot on each other? Alyx could never imagine having to ask somebody else for permission all the time, or listening to them. *Well, except Elksie.*

The thought of the woman drew a storm in her mind, and she only growled more at the man in front of her cell. He was the reason she and Nora were there, and why Elksie was dead.

The man stared awkwardly at her cell for a moment, before stammering out his reply. "I know this may be the wrong time. I wanted to apologize for what transpired. I know it won't mean anything but Elksie shouldn't have died, and-."

Alyx didn't know what her mouth was doing until she heard the scream ring out through the room. She clenched onto the bars, snapping at Mil as her muscles tensed. She wanted to lunge on him and rip his face off, but the metal prevented her from moving even an inch.

It wasn't only her screaming, however. The other prisoners were as well. The assertion that the purists ever cared, or ever didn't mean to do anything. It was so absurd, she knew they couldn't ignore it. None of them could.

Mil stumbled back, his face wide and body tense. He was like a deer in the headlights, but Alyx growled at the notion of even comparing him to the wild. She felt her eyes dilate, and the same instinct that coursed through wolves would. *Kill. Hunt. Destroy him.*

"I would kill you." She managed to bark out, and he froze, not letting himself even flinch. "I hope you and all your Purists die a painful death. I hope that one day you get to feel every single cut and bruise that you inflicted upon us. Every single life you took."

"You people think you're superior, but you're beneath us all. Even animals reject you, because they can tell what you are. Spineless creatures that betray each other for nothing, and kill not for survival, but pleasure."

The yells of the other plague backed her words, and she couldn't stop herself.

She felt her emotions settle as a cold clarity settled upon her. She didn't feel furious, she felt calculated. She was the predator, and she let her aura exude onto the man, eyes boring into him. If he wanted to apologize, he could know every horrid thing his people had done, him included.

"You destroyed a forest. You kidnapped a girl and took her to your prison camps. You killed a warrior! The one person who saw what disgusting scum you all are and left. Now you're here, begging for forgiveness? Do you know what you've done? To me? To all of us?"

Her voice got louder with every word she spoke, and her arms shook. "My mother is dead because of you." She felt the shattering in her body as the words came out. She had known it was the truth all along, but she'd never admitted it to herself, never stopped to think.

"My whole town is now a pit in the ground, families abandoning each other all for fear of their own lives. Everyone I knew is either dead or in hiding. My family left because of you, and Ravasts know if they even lived."

"Every person here has lost something because of you! You kill children and elders all while you sit on lavish thrones, then

211

come begging to us for sympathy as if you're a saint. You don't deserve pity, let alone forgiveness. Rot in hell, General Mil."

She spat out the general part as an insult, and she saw the man twitch. He was going to open his mouth, but another voice took over. It was from the lady next to her, the one who had told her about the place when she first arrived.

"I had a husband and a child once. Nobody gave a second thought to my injured arm. When your people came, you torched our whole town. You took Ana from her crib and cut her throat open, when she was only a year old. You killed my husband for daring to marry a 'plague' and took me prisoner, so I could sit and decay in these old cells."

More of the prisoners started to speak up, some weaving their own tales, and others only able to get out sobs and screams in the presence of the man. Alyx didn't speak. She didn't have to. But to think, the first time a purist would speak to them, it would be to try and beg for forgiveness. If she didn't have basic respect, she would have been the one yelling the loudest.

"Die, you hideous thing! I hope a dozen scars are carved into you so you know how it feels. Then I hope you get hung upside down and have to watch everyone you ever killed!"

"My family is dead because of you. My animals, my love, all of it, gone. I never got to meet my soulmate, never got to have children. My life is ruined because of you."

"To think you'd ask for forgiveness! As if there is any to go around. We're all going to die anyway thanks to your kind. Don't try to get empathy out of dead men."

"He wants forgiveness? Why of course! Once he agrees to let his throat be cut open. Then maybe whatever gods preside over this realm may consider giving him a drop of mercy."

The cries rang out and became a storm, and Mil continued to step back, his expression never changing. Alyx continued to watch him, letting her face scowl as she watched him. Pathetic. She knew the Purists were cowards, but not to this extent.

"Wait! Please, I don't want to kill innocents. I don't know what happened but-." He tried to get his words out, but it only infuriated everyone more.

"Leave! I'd rather have the guards here than you. You pathetic worm. You don't want to kill innocents? You have trained your whole life to do it. Monsters like you don't even deserve our time."

Mil tried to continue, "Please, no! Please." Alas, it was futile. Alyx couldn't stop herself from smirking as he backed towards the door, plague shouting at him from every corner. He was finally being confronted with the weight of his actions, and suddenly, the tough Purist was breaking apart at the seams.

It didn't take much longer for him to spin and run, darting out of the prison, his boots clamping behind him. Some of the guards creeped back in, and banged on the cells with their spears until everyone quieted down.

Alyx knew the truth though. Their voices may have quieted, but their emotions had not. Their fury would follow the purists until they all died a miserable death, and she would be the reaper.

CHAPTER 34

ARIEL

Ariel sat in her room, staring at the mirror and her glossed up face. She should have been angry at all the makeup that had been forced on her, but the revulsion wasn't there. Maybe because of what Cassor had told her.

"I don't like it either, Ariel. But, it's only one day! Once we're king and queen, we'll make the rules."

He wasn't wrong. All she had to do was wear it for the proceedings, however long that might take, then she'd never have to put on an ounce of makeup again. Still, a voice in the back of her head spoke, and not somebody else's. Her own.

She wasn't like this before. Before, she sat beside her father and supported him in court. She didn't wear makeup, and none of those elaborate dresses either. She'd talk to him about politics and court, and he'd teach her about all the noble houses.

But that was all gone now. She would see him, but they didn't talk. Instead, she'd stay by Cassor's family, and they would spray words of encouragement into her ear. It felt nice, but it wasn't the same reassuring voice as her father.

Did she have a choice in the matter, though? He had allowed her marriage to Cassor, but his distaste was clear. Cassor told her all about how he'd been looked down upon for his family. Her father was just another one of those.

"And never let yourself forget that. Once you waver, he'll have you again."

Before Ariel could agree with the voice, she jumped up as a knocking rang out. Her head shot around to look for the source, but it wasn't coming from the main door. It was coming from the servant's door. Strange. Nobody should have been coming by.

She stepped over to the door, "Who's there? I didn't call for any servants at this hour."

"It's Nemona. I wanted to talk to you."

A wave of disbelief overtook Ariel. Nemona shouldn't have been in the servants tunnels, she was a princess after all. However, it was nice to see her. She hadn't seen Nemona in a long time, and their last interaction was less than pleasant.

"Why are you here? And in the servants quarters no less? You should have come to the main door if you wanted to talk to me!"

"I was wondering if you wanted to go out. Like we used to."

Ariel froze in her tracks, not expecting the question. She supposed it wasn't uncharacteristic for Nemona, but in this situation? At the same time though, she hadn't been out for a while, and she was bored with staying in her room.

She opened the door and saw a cloaked Nemona holding a lantern. Nemona didn't say anything to her, but beckoned her into the rat infested hallway. Ariel couldn't say she didn't cringe at its condition, but it wasn't any worse than the last passageway she went down.

"Where could this take us?" After all, didn't the servant quarters only link up to other parts of the castle? But, she wouldn't have expected a hidden tunnel in the wall to lead out of the castle either.

She had to suppress a grin as she remembered the crazy adventure that led them into, and how she attacked those crazy men.

Nemona led her through the narrow corridors, and she had to walk sideways to not bump into either side. The tunnel led on and on with no turn in sight, and Ariel started to wonder if they were just going to fall out of one side of the castle.

At last, Nemonas lantern illuminated the edges of a door, and the bustling of movement could be heard on the other side. This door wasn't thick like hers, but thin and brittle, allowing all the sound to bounce out into their hall.

"Where's this?" Ariel had a few guesses, and she wondered if they were spying on their father. She did wonder what he did when he would retire to his quarters for the night.

Nemona didn't reply, and she didn't need to, as another voice spoke up. "What a bore." It was an older female voice, and Ariel's eyes began to widen, "The king can hold as many events as he wants, it's clear as day that he hates our family."

It was Burma, the mother of Cassor. Ariel had spoken to her numerous times, and she always was such a nice lady. She even gave Ariel some of her own cooking one time, and good gods, it was delicious.

But why would Nemona bring her here, and to spy on her fiance's family? What was Nemona thinking? Ariel whirled around, ready to let out a storm of words, before another familiar voice spoke up.

"Mother, there's nothing to worry about. Ariel already loves me, and she'll fight her father if she has to. Plus, the king clearly spoils her rotten. He won't argue against our marriage if she supports it."

Burma let out a huff, "If you say so dear, but the royals are vipers. I wouldn't trust a thing she says to you. She may have the royal blood, but once you're king, you need to be in control. The people will want a king in power, not a weak willed girl."

A few other members let out murmurs of agreement, but Cassor continued.

"Trust me mother, I wouldn't ever let myself be entangled by their grasps. But I can see it in her eyes- she truly is head over heels for me. I'll try to speed up the marriage as soon as I can, even if her father gives pushback. We just need her to fight him for us."

Burma let out an approving shrill, "What a smart idea, Cassor. A few anonymous notes to the king should do the trick. He'll know it's us of course, but if she is as enamored as you say she is, she'll believe whatever you say."

"Of course mother. Should I make the arrangements?"

"No need. I'll have it handled. You must congratulate your victory, son. We have been needing one for a very long time."

Ariel felt her brain about to burst. She knew it was them, their voices were the same, but their words were not. She tried to replay the conversation in her head, to grasp what they were saying, but it all led her to one truth.

Cassor never loved her. He approached her on that fateful night because he knew she'd run out of the ball. He knew that his family needed support, and he saw her as an easy target. But she'd been one, hadn't she?

She had fallen in love with Cassor, but she couldn't find that tingly feeling in her chest anymore. Instead, she felt cold ashes, frozen over like the depths of hell.

They continued to speak, but the words zoned out. Nemona tried to say something as well, but she only felt a ringing in her ears. How could this happen again? And now of all times? Couldn't she just be happy for once?

She spun around, hitting the sides of the wall as she tried to break into a sprint, not caring as the stone scraped against her flesh. She couldn't have found her door sooner, slamming through it as tears poured down her eyes.

Her legs fell under her and she hit the rug, curling into a ball as her chest heaved, a scream erupting from her throat. Snot and tears mixed together into a disgusting mess on the floor, and she tried to push herself up, only to let out another horrid scream.

She didn't know how long she was like that, until the door opened and a voice spoke. "Ariel? What's wrong? Ariel?"

It should have been a comforting voice, oh it should have been. But now the soft tone was sickly sweet. No, it had turned bitter, because it wasn't a boy speaking to her, but a monster.

Her hands turned to fists and she worked up the nerve to let out another scream. He tried to approach her, but she surged up. "Don't you dare get closer! Don't you even try to use that stupid voice on me! I know what you did. You used me!"

Cassor tried to feign shock, but Ariel could see beneath his mask. Desperation hit his eyes, and he reached his hands out. "What are you talking about Ariel? What happened? Please, talk to me."

Ariel reached for the nearest thing, a brush, and threw it at his head. "You know what happened! And you couldn't care less. Get out, before I rip you to shreds!"

He tried to make one more pathetic attempt at soothing her, but she had enough. She felt fury wade through her veins, and a sick voice came to her mind.

"Make him pay for what he did to. Let him suffer."

Sadness didn't plague her eyes when she rose again, but cold hatred. That seemed to be enough to scare him off, because before she could approach him, tearing her fingers into his skin, he ran the other way.

Ariel should have followed him, but she couldn't. The anger fled her as quick as it came, and she fell to the floor again. Her father was gone, Nemona was gone, and now Cassor was too.

She had her crown, her riches, and her throne. But now, she felt the same as she did so many years ago. A little girl watching her room being filed away, and her family gone.

CHAPTER 35

ALYX

The guards had left their posts unmanned. Alyx didn't know why, or for how long, but she took her chance and lunged. She yanked the door open, leaving it ajar as she studied her surroundings.

"What are you doing?" One plague yelled, and others began to rise up and stare at her. What was in their eyes? Hope? Satisfaction? She couldn't tell. She wanted to break them all out then, but she couldn't.

She needed to find Nora, and she couldn't sneak everyone out. "Please!" One begged, and they began to bang on their bars. She heard a shout in the distance, and she gritted her teeth. She looked at them all, staring right into their eyes.

"I'll come back. I promise." Some moaned with dread, but Alyx couldn't pay them anymore mind. She ran out the hallway, darting towards the one on her left. She hugged the walls, watching for any shadows, or hiding places.

The barren hallways offered no escape if she was caught, and she knew they wouldn't make the same mistake twice. This was becoming a matter of life or death. She recalled all that she had given to get there. What she still would give.

If she was caught now, every single plague would be a prisoner. Nora would become a Purist, and Elksie would be rolling in her grave, no doubt. But most of all, she couldn't tell the others. She wouldn't stop the Purists. This would happen for generations to come.

She couldn't risk all that, so she trudged forward, ready to tear out the throat of anyone that came near. This wasn't their territory anymore. It was hers, and they dare not cross it.

She came to an intersection, with four paths awaiting her. She knew nothing of any of them, but her head snapped to the right. Something drew her mind forward then, something she could only equate to pure instinct.

She bolted down the marble floors, letting air rush by her, her tunic whooshing behind her. She came to a halt, when only then, did she see the giant door looming over her. Her eyes fell, for she recognized one of the symbols on it.

She remembered when she was a girl, and a woman told her a story. How a griffin would part the heavens, and there it was, carved into the door. Next to it was another creature, one she couldn't know, but still majestic in its own right.

She hesitated as her hands brushed the door, like she was touching an old artifact. But the door parted for her, and she slipped in the small crack, looking at the looming hallway in front of her. She was never afraid of anything, but for some reason, the room humbled her.

Her next few steps carried her into an office, with a wooden desk being the first thing to greet her eyes. To either side, shelves were held, whole stacks of books in them. She cringed, reading was a skill she did not possess.

But another sense took the better of her. This whole room, it was a rich flaunt. Gold was sitting as if it wasn't valuable, and elaborate treasures were hidden in every corner. It should be burned for all she cared, not sitting here as a useless trinket.

"Plague."

She whipped around, and a figure was in the hallway. The one who had been plaguing her at her cell, who watched as she was brought in. Who she had heard the other plague refer to as the 'Purist' in fear.

She hid her face behind a mask, detailed to look identical to a human face. Golden and white robes spilled from her, and she took two steps forward. A challenge.

"Stay back, you disgusting Purist!" She grabbed for the nearest thing, a book, and flung it at her, but the purist only side-stepped the blow.

"Hasty, hasty. You barge into my office, and now assault me? Even a plague should have better manners than that."

Any formalities were dropped, and Alyx could see what she projected now. Pure hatred, as if Alyx had killed her entire family, all in front of her. It was something she should have been wearing, not this Purist.

"Call your guards already. Or do you think you can fight me alone?" She would like to beat up the Purist, destroying her in front of everyone, just so they could see how pitiful she really was.

But something about that encounter was off, like why she approached her to begin with. She should be tied up by now, in a cell. This Purist, she was toying with her. She had to be.

"Always so eager to fight, are you? No, I wish to have a civilized discussion. Though I see how that could be difficult for you. Please, sit."

Alyx didn't move to do anything, and neither did the Purist. She didn't know what she was on, to think that she'd let herself be vulnerable. As if.

"You are quite a curious plague, you know? Transfixing my commander's interest so easily. Knowing the names of my Purists, and of me. Then coming into this room, of every room in the temple."

"Make your point." Alyx raised her fists, ready to deliver a blow right to the Purists face.

"Have you been hearing voices as of late, plague? Do think carefully."

Alyx froze, her fists lowering as she thought back. *How could she have known?* All in that fateful day at the marketplace, where everything changed. She talked to Elksie and Nora, and the purists found her. And she heard the voice for the first time.

"Ah. So you have been hearing them. I suppose I should have known. That Ravast always knew how to make things difficult."

Ravast? The old legend? Now she was sure this woman was crazy. She thought a Ravast was speaking into her head, helping her? She couldn't make room for fantasies in her life. No, there was only the hard reality around her.

"I'm afraid it's quite real."

Her head shot over, because now she could hear the source of the voice. Her eyes met a statue, and one of a griffin, perpetually locked in a state of attack. But she only jumped when its eyes rolled back to look at her.

"What- what are you doing, you witch? This isn't real!" She shouted at the Purist, distancing herself from the two of them.

"You're right. It shouldn't be. A Ravast, the Purity in its finest form, choosing something like you. Helping you avoid my authorities, after everything I've done for it."

She approached Alyx, making a steady pace towards her. "But it ends now. I will not allow another hurdle to my plans arise."

"Don't let her touch you! Run!"

Alyx dived to the left as the Purist leaned down to reach her, her gloves now removed from her hands. Alyx didn't know what she was trying to do, but decided she didn't want to find out. The griffin gave her a final glance, before a scream sounded in her mind.

"Touch me. Now!"

Alyx had a split second decision, staring at the hand of the approaching Purist. No. She would never take her chances with them. She spun around, leaping for the statue, her fingers grazing its cold stone surface.

At once, a crack formed on the statue, then another. The Purist let out a shriek, falling to her knees as she cried. "What have you done!?" If there was any demon here, it was her.

The cracks grew larger and larger, until finally, Alyx felt a force throwing her back, and a light shined out, blinding anything she could see. Her back hit the desk, and she let out a cry of pain, hearing the shuffling of things as they got thrown back.

When she opened her eyes, she wasn't staring at the ceiling, but the sky. She looked to her side, and the wall was gone, only an open gaping hole in its place.

When she looked to her other side, the Purist had been knocked back, and so had her mask. The Purist sat up in a hurry, and Alyx saw what she tried to hide so dearly.

Her face had an awful scar going across it, but not just any scar. Claw marks. Huge ones at that, which completely cut through her eyes, and most of her face.

She scrambled to get her mask back, and Alyx felt a pang of horror. The same scars this woman would condemn others to die for, she held on her very face.

But that wasn't what drew her eyes finally. No, instead, the massive form in the corner did. Half in the destroyed building and half out of it, a griffin stood.

It threw its wings out, letting a cry of victory ring out for the whole world to hear. But that was when Alyx saw its coat. It was completely white, with bright red eyes. It looked exactly like her, and Alyx was unable to look away.

"Hurry! We must leave!"

Right on cue, a whole squadron of Purists burst through the door, led by him. Her face twisted into a scowl as her eyes bore into him. She wanted him dead.

"Get that plague! Now!" He shouted and the squadron descended on them, but the griffin moved just as fast. The first two attackers were flung back as the griffin slashed at their chests, blood oozing off them.

"But- Nora!" She couldn't leave her here, let the purists brainwash her and inflict whatever poison they had in store. The griffin gave her a look, and Alyx felt her blood go cold. At once, she could see how this would end.

She would die, and Nora would be a Purist forever. The griffin would once more be stone, and the Purist would have her way. Which of the two evils did she have to pick?

"Archers!" Deciding to stay clear of the griffin, a few Purists drew bows on them, and Alyx gritted her teeth, running for the griffin.

"I'm sorry Nora!" She cried, hoping somehow Nora could hear it, in whatever room she was in. She stared at the griffin, grabbing hold of its feathers as she struggled to yank herself up. The griffin shook to the side, jostling her onto its back.

At once, its wings veered up, and they were off the ground. A sudden wave of sickness overtook her, and she hung onto the feathers of the creature for dear life. An arrow whizzed by them, and the griffin turned, flying up and away.

"Fire!" It was the screams of Benjamin once more, but another voice overtook him.

"No. Let them go." It was the Purist, who now stood in the entrance of the hole.

"Are you mad? Letting a plague escape!" Such blatant disrespect surprised Alyx, but she shouldn't have been. Even animals had respect in their ranks, but the purists were below that.

"Every problem has a fix my dear Benjamin, and this one will as well. Only time can tell." A sinister note was added to the words, but at that point, their voices got too muffled to hear.

Alyx watched as the purist temple became a dot in the distance, and she let out a sigh, looking at the horizon ahead.

—

When they landed in a forest, Alyx got off right away, hugging the ground as she let the situation hit her. She had left Nora, and she would need to go back there and get her. She turned to the griffin, her fists clenched.

"You better have a way to get her back! Or this is going to be your fault!"

The griffin let its face drop, moving to stretch its leg out. "Do not fear, wildling. We will get your friend back, and we will stop the purists. I would not have chosen you if I expected anything less."

Alyx narrowed her eyes, "And how do you plan to do that?"

The griffin turned its head to the south, "I have heard many things while I was in the purists office. A rebellion of plague goes to the south. We shall go there."

A rebellion? Of plague? A light filled her chest at the thought. If they could somehow overtake the purists, things could be good once again.

She shifted, looking to the griffin, realizing she had yet to know its name, or well, anything about it. "Who are you? And I mean beyond the obvious."

"I go by many names, but you may call me Anzonia. As for the rest, well, I can tell you on the way." At that, Anzonia beckoned her onto its back again, before taking off into the sky.

CHAPTER 36

MIL

Mil had traveled before, but somehow, this time it was different. The mountains seemed to ward them off at every turn, and the men were going weary. Not just with the mountains though, but with him.

He didn't want to go either, but what was he meant to do with the Purist? He felt his stomach drop as he remembered her words again, but did it matter? He could disagree with her all he wanted, but it wouldn't do anything.

Anita continued to talk with him, as did some of the others, but Bolios maintained a hard stance. He was sure Bolios didn't hate him, or at least that was what he wanted to believe, but a wall had formed between them. No matter what he did, Bolios kept that wall up.

As they got closer and closer, Mil tried to remember what came before this mess. He felt so happy then, learning the lessons of the purists, speaking with her, and hanging out with Bolios. Sure, they were strict at times, but he never found himself doubting them. Ever since he was general though, things were different.

The plague weren't the ghoulish monsters he thought they were. The purists were not as kind either. These weren't new thoughts to him, but it was the first time he could think them without any guilt either.

But he was too late. Even if he did think that, wasn't he too far in now? Hadn't he already pulled away from Bolios? How was he even meant to begin to fix it? How was he meant to defy the purists?

"We're here!" It was Anita, and the whole party halted as they came to a giant cave-in. He could see the cracks of something, but it was buried amidst many boulders. God, how were they going to get through there? Was the Purist sure there was something of value here?

He let out a sigh, "Get some of the carts out, we'll have to pick the rocks off."

Muttering broke out behind him, "Is this even worth it? Picking apart a whole mountain just because something might be in there?"

Another voice joined in, "And what will they even use it for? Did you see what happened last time we were sent on a hunt?"

Finally, Bolios stepped forward. "We aren't doing this."

Mil froze, but Anita spun around right away. "Excuse me? Must I remind you that you aren't the second anymore, Bolios?" She nudged her elbow into him, and he reluctantly spun around.

"I don't need to be second to say this. This is absurd. First, we're expected to murder innocents, and now, we need to shovel out boulders, just because there might be something of value? Would you even care if those boulders crushed all of us?"

Anita shot back, "Quit your worrying. All I hear is blasphemy against the Purist. Why are you even here if you question her orders? You're no better than the plague we eradicate!"

Bolios turned his gaze to Mil, but he couldn't meet Bolios's eyes. "Bolios, stop this, please. If the boulders get too unsteady, we'll find another way." He knew that wasn't possible though. Anything they did could lead to a rock slide.

Bolios held his gaze for a bit longer, before he backed up. Part of the group split to follow him, and suddenly, their party was split down the middle. Bolios gave one last look to him, "Don't do this, Mil."

Mil wanted to scream out then, to tell him he agreed, and that the purists were wrong, but no words came out. Instead, Anita spoke for him.

"You're all traitors! I can't believe you were ever Purists to begin with. Scum like you is what corrupts the order!"

The sickening sound of scraping metal was heard as everyone started to draw their blades, pointing them at each other like they weren't all brothers and sisters.

Mil didn't want to, but he drew his sword. He knew what was going to happen, and he couldn't do anything about it.

Everything was a flash from there, swords hitting one another as screams flew. Blood splattered the stone field, and it was as if everyone's faces blurred. They weren't people, just things on the battlefield.

It only hit him when his sword came against Bolios's what he was doing. Bolios didn't say anything to him, only flashed him angry eyes as he drew his sword, ready to slice his neck. What came next was only natural for Mil. Or at least he hoped it was only natural.

He flung his sword out, and it hit the soft belly of Bolios. Blood sprayed, and Bolios stumbled back as his sword fell, body hitting the ground.

Mil stared at the body as he convulsed, eyes staring at Mil like he'd just torn his heart out. Mil let his sword fall, his ears ringing as the fighting around him blurred into one symphony.

A scream erupted from his throat as he tried to remember what had led them to this point, before a greater sound took over. The rocks of the cave began to fall apart, spewing in all sorts of directions. The fighting paused as people jumped to get out of the way, and a huge shadow emerged.

"I've been waiting to finally meet you, Mil."

The eyes of a giant beast, part lion, part man, stared right back at him.

CHAPTER 37

ARIEL

She stormed to her room, tears falling from her face. She was so stupid. Of course Cassor was too good to be true. He only wanted her because she was the princess. He wanted riches for his family, not her.

And she had rebuked her father, and her sister, all for what? How was she going to apologize, rectify this? And now who was she going to marry? It was all too much, and she was on the verge of breaking down right there and then.

"Bessa!" She called as she came to her room, finding it rather empty. She searched the extra rooms, but found nothing. Now her handmaiden was disappearing as well? She let out a cry of fury as she went to search for her, smelling a putrid scent as she went.

Did the maids not clean properly? The castle never smelt like that. She followed it to its source, opening up the door to the sunroom. She knew it well, as it was where she had decided to place her gift, the statue.

But as she opened it, she was met with a trail of blood. Her eyes followed it, until they landed on Bessa, laid on the ground, life drained from her eyes. Her throat had been slit, but she had various other injuries all over her. Likely all before death.

Ariel jumped back, fear racking her as she looked around her. Who could have done this? And why? Bessa was only a handmaiden. Nobody would have any reason to kill her.

She heard screams from down the hall, and the clanging of steel. Something wasn't right. Where were all the guards? And where was her father?

She made to run down to her right, but she froze when she saw a figure there. A woman, middle aged, and with bright ginger hair. A bloodied sword hung at her side, and it hit Ariel right away. That was Bessas blood.

But the woman also had golden cloaks, one that Ariel knew. This wasn't any person. This was a Purist, and she was in the palace. "Who are you?" She already knew the answer, but she backed up, her legs aching to flee.

The woman smiled at her. "Trisha. Commander Trisha. And you're Princess Ariel, I presume?"

Ariel didn't give her a reply, and instead, turned to run. But the Commander was faster, and next thing she knew, she was slammed back into the room Bessa was in.

She backed up as much as she could, shoes going into wet blood as she stepped over her handmaiden's body. Trisha followed her in, staying near the door, never once retracting her sword.

"Where is your sister, princess? Tell me, and I may let you go."

Ariel couldn't tell her if she wanted to. But her mind was focused on other matters. She wanted to find her sister? And what about her father? She prayed they were okay, though she knew her prayers should really be on herself right about now.

"She's in her room!" She wasn't even sure if Nemona had a room, though surely she had to. Trisha observed her, before continuing to approach. "Stop!"

"You can't lie to me, Princess. We'll find your weed of a sister either way."

Trisha started to close the gap, and Ariel ran to the side, near the window. Maybe if she could only open it, she could jump off. *And fall to her death.*

She begged for any reprieve from the situation, banging on the panged glass as hard as she could. That was until she felt a sharp pain in her back.

Her legs toppled over themselves, and she heard a shatter as the glass broke on impact, and she fell to the ground below, shards falling over her.

Her hair unraveled into a mess, tinged with blood as it spilled down her back. She looked up to her attacker, who stood over her, blade ready.

Her eyes drifted to the glass shard that was nearby her, arm reaching up to grab it.

"Do it. Now."

Trisha paused all of a sudden, turning to face the wyvern statue that was in the middle of the hall. Ariel was frozen, trying to solve the situation, but she had never been prepared for it.

"Do it!" The voice screamed louder in her head, and with all the resolve she mustered, she gripped the glass as hard as she could and launched up.

Trisha looked down, but it was too late, and the shard slashed across her throat, blood spurting out. Her attacker let out a few gasps, stepping back as she tried to say something. Anything.

She fell down, trying to keep her balance as blood continued to flow. Ariel couldn't care less, trying instead to keep her focus on staying awake. She was also bleeding, and at this point, she had no idea how much.

Is this where I die? She absently wondered, thinking about everything that could be, and likely wouldn't. Everyone was gone. The palace was empty. Who was going to find her?

Perhaps her mind called for someone, as then two guards burst through the door.

"Princess!" One called, sitting her up, while the other checked her attacker, presumably to see if they were dead. "Princess, you must come, it's your father!"

All her dizziness fled at that sentence.

—

He was laying on a bed, bandages wrapped around him, his form faintly moving. She had learned what had happened while waiting there. The Purists had launched an attack on the palace, and her father had bravely fought them off, but been injured.

She also had been seen to, but she couldn't care less about that. The healers said her father was in a coma, and they didn't know when he'd wake.

Her concentration was only broken when a figure came through the door. She was ready to tell them to go away, until she saw who it was. Nemona.

She shot up, running to her and hugging her before she could get any words out. "You're alive!" She cried, letting new tears shed from her face. She had thought her sister dead, as nobody could find her, but she was wrong. She was still here.

Nemona didn't know how to react, staring at her blankly as she pulled back. It was only then that she realized something. Nemona was a stunning image of their father, her black hair, sharp features, and hazel eyes. Not to mention her height.

"What happened to you?" Nemona asked, looking at the bandages that were draped across her back. Ariel shrugged it off, preferring not to detail any of the events. She was more focused on her sister still being alive.

She turned to her father, drooping her head. "He's in a coma. The healers don't know when he'll wake up. I don't know what to do, Nemona."

Nemona sat down at a chair, resting her head on her fist as she watched their father. "He'll make it."

Ariel didn't know how she knew, but it comforted her nonetheless, despite Nemonas pensive state. It was then that a crowd of nobles shot through the door, being led by the king's advisor.

"Princess Ariel, Nemona." He greeted, bowing his head to the both of them. "I am so sorry to hear about your father, we all give our deepest condolences."

Ariel knew they couldn't care less, and she glared at them, which gave them all pause. They should get down to why they were actually here already.

"But, with him indisposed, someone else is going to have to take over the throne. As the named heir, you are first in line to take it. Yet, we understand this is a heavy burden."

Her blood ran cold.

"As such, we'll be sure to appoint the appropriate noble to guide you." The noble bowed, trying to hide the smile etching its way onto his face.

Ariel had no words. All of this happens, and their first thought is to secure their own power? She didn't even want to take the throne with all that happened, but was this any better?

"And with this attack, the people will need answers. Until we can find a regent, I'm sure you can handle that, no?" His smirk only widened as he gazed at her, but she didn't respond.

Ariel tuned out the rest of his words, letting only the weight of the situation fall upon her.

—

Ariel was in her best dress, a crown seated on her head as she looked down at the mob of people she was presenting to. A bead of sweat dripped down her forehead as she readied her voice, advisors and guards standing at either side of her.

"People of Evalkyr, although I'm sure it worries you, none of you should pay any mind to the recent attack on the palace. My father is recovering, and soon will be out to meet you personally. But until then, I will have to take his place."

A roar came from the crowd, as one prominent voice took hold. "And what about the purists? They come into our land, attack the palace, and you'll let them? This is Arbornail all over again!"

Ariel tried to calm them, ushering out words, but they were drowned out by the yells of the crowd. The advisors leaned down to whisper into her ears, but she ignored both of them, stress overwhelming her mind.

"No, we will do something about the purists! We just don't know what yet!"

More mutters broke out, "Hear that? The princess doesn't know! What a good system of leadership! Who even said a woman should be in charge to begin with?"

Ariel had no words to compete with him, because even she wasn't sure. It was true, she really didn't know how to approach the situation, and needed her fathers guidance.

"Let go. Ignore them. Focus only on yourself."

Ariel listened. She let a flood of emotions overwhelm her, and at last, she let out a scream, everyone turning to see what it was about. A burst of power came from her in, and a boom sounded. But it wasn't in her head.

A chunk of the castle was blown out, and a giant mass emerged from it. A roar sounded, and the people all began to rush back, as no, it couldn't be. A dragon?

It flew towards them at alarming speeds, and Ariel could only watch as it landed on the platform, guards and advisors alike jumping off to avoid it. Only she remained, watching as it towered over her.

It did nothing at first, until at last, it smiled, before turning its head up, towards the people. It opened its maw, and a burst of lightning shot forward, going right into the crowd.

A scream was heard, then a dozen people were killed on the spot, and others fled to avoid the beast's rage.

Ariel didn't know how to feel, but she did know one thing. She liked it when they weren't yelling at her. A little bit too much.

"Exactly. Just the way it should be."

www.ingramcontent.com/pod-product-compliance
Lightning Source LLC
Chambersburg PA
CBHW022113240626
47153CB00007B/2344